TAKING HER DOWN

SAVAGE BROTHERS MC—2ND GENERATION

JORDAN MARIE

Cover Designer by: Wicked By Design

WARNING: This book contains sexual situations, violence and other adult themes. Recommended for 18 and above.

Created with Vellum

Keanna Estrada, my own Kee-Kee. I hope you enjoy being a part of this one. Love you!

And to my granddaughter, maybe you always be strong, love fiercely, forgive carefully, life fully, and always—ALWAYS—stand on your own two feet and breathe in that independence every single day. You are my heart.

J

She was a fire in his blood and he was going to have her.

No matter the cost.

The Savage Brothers MC is one of the most ruthless clubs around. Dragon, the club president, is not a man you want on your bad side.

Dylan "Chains" Allen wanted Kayden West more than he ever wanted anything in his life.

In his world, when you wanted something you took it.

So, he did.

He knows there will be hell to pay. You don't mess with Dragon's daughter and survive.

But, some things are worth the price you have to pay.

If taking Kayden is what is finally going to drag him down to hell, then he'll just make sure he enjoys the ride.

Welcome back to the world of the Savage Brothers MC. We might be talking the second generation, but that doesn't mean our boys are put out to pasture. They're still bad, they're still hot and they're still going to get your motor revving. It's just that the second generation might be even dirtier, grab a fan and a cold bottle of water. It's going to be a hot summer.

1

KAYDEN

"Girl, your brother is *fine.*"

I roll my eyes at Keanna. I love her, she's my girl, but she's a nut. It's also a little creepy that she's mackin' on my big brother. All the girls do. They look at Dom and by the way they fall down on their knees around him, you'd think he's the second coming.

I don't see it. Then again, if they lived with my brothers, they probably wouldn't either. Dom and Thomas are both pigs. I love them, but more times than not I want to kill them. There's just four years between Thomas and I and five with Dom, but that doesn't matter. I'm forever trapped as their *little* sister. They don't care that I'm eighteen and moving out on my own. They're worse than my father.

Okay, that's not exactly true either. My dad nearly had a stroke when I told him I was moving out into my own apartment. Mom did her best to calm him down, but even she had problems containing him with this. There's a reason people call my father Dragon. He reacts fiercely—especially when it's about someone he cares about. And, oh yeah, he can definitely breathe fire so hot that it burns everything and everyone around him.

Usually I don't complain. My old man has been the best dad a girl could have. I never once doubted he loved me. He stays hella busy and despite the fact that he doesn't look like the soccer dad, or the dad of a cheerleader, I can't name one game that I played in, or cheered at that my old man—and half the club and a couple other clubs—hadn't been at.

I'm treated like a princess. That's what most of them call me. Of course, I'm a biker princess and that changes everything. You see, my father is Detroit *Dragon* West, president and founder of the Savage Brothers Motorcycle Club. If you haven't heard of the Savage Brothers, you've probably been living under a rock. They carry more weight around these parts than law enforcement. Hell, half of the police are on my father's payroll—not that I'm supposed to know that kind of thing.

The club is all about the men. Women usually only have two roles. You're either a Twinkie or an old lady. That's it and that's not the lifestyle I want. Don't get me wrong, my mom has lived this life and she rocks at being an old lady. She's right too. Men might want to think they have all the power, but my dad would give her anything she asks for and if she's really against something, she usually manages to get her way.

My brothers are all about the club. Dominic and Thomas are both prospects for the club now. Dad's not cutting them any slack. They won't ride his coattails at all. They have to prove themselves to the other members. I thought that was harsh and Mom didn't necessarily agree either, but Dom—strangely enough—wanted it that way. I'm not sure what Thomas wanted. He and Dom are so tight that I think he'd follow Dom to the ends of the earth without questioning him at all.

I, on the other hand, want to live on my own. I want a nice normal guy who's not jumping on his bike at three in the morning to do my father's bidding. I want a guy that won't have to go through hell just to be mine—and trust me if I ever picked a guy in the club he'd have to go through some crazy shit. He still might, even if he's not in the club. That's the curse of being a biker princess. It has perks, but the drawbacks are plenty.

"Oh, my fuck. He's taking his shirt off. Take it off baby and Keanna will come over there and lick every delicious inch of that milk chocolate body."

"Keanna! Knock it off, you ho!" I growl, shoving her so hard she loses her balance and her hip slides against her car.

"What? That man is fine!"

"It's my brother you're talking about. That's just grossy-gross."

"Let me just say if that was the view in my house every morning, moving out would be the last fucking thing I'd want to do."

"Again, he's my *brother* and you're weird. Put this in your trunk and I'll run back in and get the last box."

"I got it, Sis," Thomas says and I turn around smiling at him.

I love Thomas so much—I love both of my brothers. They're as different as night and day. Dom is silent, more self-assured and definitely more controlling. Thomas is laid back, sweet and funny and even a little bit shy. Thomas has a stutter that he's worked hard to overcome. It's still noticeable when he's upset or the center of attention. I think he gets embarrassed by it, but he'd never admit to that. No one would dare comment on it either—especially if Dom is around.

"Thanks, Tom. You can still move out with me you know!"

"Pledgin' the club, Kay-Kay" he reminds me, using the nickname he gave me over fifteen years ago when I'd climb up in his lap and hang upside down over his legs, watching cartoons.

"Whatever. I'm going to miss you," I tell him, honestly.

He pulls me into his arms and hugs me tight. I wrap my arms around him, close my eyes and breathe his scent in deep as we embrace.

"Love you," he whispers.

"Love you too, Tom," I respond just as quietly.

"Hey, where's mine," Dom growls in his deep voice. I pull out of Tom's arms to look up at him and laugh. I take the shirt he has slung over his shoulder and throw it back at him.

"Put your shirt on before Keanna trips over her own tongue."

"Hey, I'm just admiring the goods. Don't you listen to her Dom, baby. It'd be a crime to wrap that chocolate bar back up," she flirts.

Dom just shakes his head at Keanna, but he puts his shirt on —and I'm grateful.

"I'm going to miss you too, Dom," I tell him and give him a hug.

"Is Dad going to hand me my ass when he discovers you moved out while him and Mom are gone for Aunt Dani's birthday party?"

"Oh stop. You know yourself Dad and Mom checked out my apartment last week and gave me the okay before they left."

"Yeah, but I don't think Dad realized you were planning on moving this quick," Tom grumbles.

"It's not my fault the previous tenant moved out a month earlier than expected. It'd be silly to let the place stay empty when I'm dying to move into it!"

"I still don't think Dad is going to be happy," Dom warns.

He's right of course. Dad may have agreed to me moving out, but I'm sure he thought he would work on talking me out of it, while I lived at home for another month. I don't tell Dom that however.

"You two going to come have dinner with me in my new digs Saturday?"

"Are you cooking?" Dom laughs.

I roll my eyes. I can't boil water and we all know it—they just never let me forget it.

"I thought we could order pizza," I laugh.

"In that case, sure."

"Do it Friday," Keanna whines. "I have to work Saturday."

"Saturday it is," Dom responds.

I shake my head at him as Keanna huffs.

"That's not nice," I scold him.

"Your girl is a freak," Dom replies back.

"A freak in the sheets," Keanna says, sticking her tongue out. "You'd be so lucky, chocolate drop," she adds as she walks around to the driver's side door.

"I'm a one-woman man, Kee-Kee and she's already in place," Dom laughs.

"I don't see a ring on your hand," Keanna grumbles.

"It's complicated," Dom responds, with a shrug.

"Because you're afraid of her Dad?" I whisper where only Dom can hear me.

"Let it go, Sis."

"You wait much longer and you'll have competition," I warn him, louder this time.

"From... From ... who?" Tom asks, surprisingly he stutters, something he rarely does these days unless he's upset.

I look at him surprised to see the alarm on his face. Is the reason Dom hasn't made a move on Gabby because Thomas likes her?

Yikes. That's a whole other can of worms.

"Brandon Lavers," I answer.

"Where'd you hear this?" Dom says, his voice as menacing as any I've heard my father use.

"Saw him putting the moves on her today at Weavers, while her and Jazz were eating."

"We'll see about that," he growls and starts to walk away.

"Dom don't get into trouble..."

"We'll see you at dinner Saturday," he responds, not bothering to look at me. I slide into Keanna's car, frowning.

"I think you just bought Brandon an old-fashioned ass whoopin', girl."

I look at Keanna and sigh.

"You might be right. I should probably call and warn Gabby."

"Warn her that she's about to have three men fighting over her? That lucky bitch don't need a warning. She needs us to bring her a bottle of wine that we all can drink while enjoying the show," Keanna says with her usual snark.

"Let's just go get the last of my shit in the apartment, can we?"

"I guess, but my idea is better," she mutters, starting up her vehicle.

"Whatever," I respond, thinking I really better check in with Gabby later. I don't get a good feeling about the tension I saw on Thomas's face. If her and Dom aren't careful, they could really hurt him.

2

CHAINS

I pull into the parking lot of a small dive bar called The Den. It doesn't stand out. It's got brown wood siding, a neon sign standing high in a graveled parking lot, and a bouncer sitting at the front door. You could find the same exact place in any town, U.S.A. Hell, I've probably been in most of them. The only thing different about this one is that I'll be crashing in the back room for a couple of weeks.

I called in a favor from a buddy of mine I once served under, when I was just getting started in the military. He belongs to a club in Tennessee—The Savage Brothers. I spent a couple of weeks there while the President took his old lady and kids to some beach for a few weeks. Good club, good brothers, but I got restless.

Gunner cleared the way for me to stay here in Kentucky for a few more weeks. They have a parent chapter here. I've spent my time out of service moving from one club to the next, but that's how I live my life. I don't really have a need to put roots down. I should have gone by the Savage Clubhouse and announced myself, but I'm too fucking tired. I'll do it tomorrow. They gave me the okay to stay there, but when Gunner mentioned the room here, I jumped on that. I like being alone. It's one of the reasons I haven't joined a club.

I need to figure out what the fuck I'm doing. I'm at a crossroads and the only thing I really know is that I'm not going back into the military. Still, at thirty, working a week here and a week there probably is not a good game plan. Then again, there's no one counting on me, but me, so it's not like it matters.

This is not how I once saw my life. Nearing thirty, no kids, no old lady, nothing holding me down anywhere. When I first went into the service, I didn't do it to be patriotic. I did it because it was honest income and I had a woman to provide for. I don't know that I ever loved Angie—some days she could be a pure bitch, especially when I came home early on leave and found her sucking off my Lt. Colonel. Seeing that does things to a man. Doesn't matter if you love the bitch, she was yours and she let another man touch her. She took another man's dick into what I deemed my territory. After that, I didn't much give a fuck about anything. I did my time, got out and I've been rambling around ever since.

That's how I got my road name. Chains. Assholes thought it'd be funny to name me opposite of the thing I craved the most —*freedom*. I like it though.

There are days I feel like I need a place to hang my hat every night and come off the road. Then, I remember I don't wear a fucking hat.

I shut down Betty, climb off and manage not to groan as the kinks in my back snap, crackle and pop louder than any breakfast cereal.

By the time I make it over to the bouncer, he's arguing with a sexy little minx with legs so long they make my dick stand up and take notice. She's a curvy thing too, with an ass to make a man beg and boobs to make him kill. She's got soft curled hair that's all natural and a dark black, that still somehow shines in the moonlight. It's her skin that grabs my attention. It's a creamy mocha that makes me want to lick every inch of it. It's smooth, unblemished and appears soft as silk. I have trouble tearing my gaze away from it. That's when I truly take in her face and realize I need to get my dick under control. This chick is young.

Jailbait young.

"Come on, Nailer. You know yourself Dad gave me the job here."

"He did. He also made it damn clear you are only to work during the day, Kayden."

"I just want to go in and pick up the paperwork. I won't be in there long."

"Not happening. There's a club party going on in there tonight. Dragon would have my ass if I let you in."

"Christ, it's not like I haven't seen a club party, Nailer."

"Seeing one when it's just starting and being there when it's in full swing are two different kettles of fish. Not happening, Kayden."

"Just let me in to get the paperwork and that's it. You can walk in front of me and hide me from the big bad party."

"No thanks, I choose life. Your old man might have some years on him, and Nic has definitely mellowed him, but there's no fucking way I'm going to cross him."

"Whatever. I can't believe this. I swear you're all dead set on treating me like I'm still a baby for the rest of my life."

The man just shrugs at the girl's outburst.

"I'm not a little girl!" she huffs, sounding like the very thing she's denying.

"You are to me," the man she called Nailer, responds.

"Do I look like a little girl to you?" the girl asks, surprising the fuck out of me. She's staring right at me, her eyes as dark as her hair. *Jesus.* She's sex served on a plate and wrapped up with a fuck-me-and-spend-your-life-in-jail bow.

I grunt, mostly because I want to tell her she does look like a little girl, but I still want to fuck her.

Her perfectly formed eyebrow, thick and curved as if kissed by the damn gods, arches up in question, all while the other remains perfectly still on her face. It doesn't move at all. I don't know why I notice that, but fuck me, I do. I couldn't tell you why I like it... but it turns me on.

"Who are you? You don't look like a member of the Savage crew."

She reaches out then, her hand moving over my cut, a finger reaching up to move over the rocker panel with my name on it. It's stupid. There's no way I can feel the heat of her touch—at least logically, but yet somehow, I do.

"He's not one of ours," Nailer answers and he goes to stand between me and the girl.

I don't let him—which is stupid. Instead, I reach out and grab the girl's hand, holding it to my chest. Her hand is much smaller than mine. Mine is stark white and inked, but it stands out against her soft, slightly darker one. She feels delicate and gentle, something I've never had... *not once in my life.*

"Chains," she says, still looking at my name. Slowly her gaze travels up to me.

"That's my name," I tell her.

"Are you going to let go of my hand?" she asks.

"Do you want me to?" I respond.

For some reason that makes her smile and as I watch those full lips stretch into a smile, I find I like that even more than the sound of my name on her tongue.

"Kayden, get behind me," Nailer orders.

"Are you going to let me into my office?" she asks, not turning her gaze away from me.

"No fucking way," Nailer growls.

"Then, I think I'll pass," she shrugs, lifting her shoulders up as if she doesn't have a care in the world and this time it's me who smiles.

"You here to join the Savage Brothers, nomad?" she asks, surprising me. Apparently, whoever the girl is, she's damn familiar with the club life. She looks too soft to be part of my world, of any biker's world, and for some reason the thought of her losing that bothers me.

"Nope, not me."

"Too bad. You might pretty the place up."

"Not much pretty about me, Baby Girl."

"I think I'm a better judge of that than you," she says with a grin.

"If you want to stay in town alive, you best let go of Kayden."

"She yours?" I ask, still not taking my eyes off her—and still not letting her go.

"Ew, no way," the girl responds, crinkling her face up.

"You don't need to be making that kind of face damn it. Before I claimed my old lady—"

"Oh, don't get your balls in a twist. I just meant you diapered me when I was little. The thought of us… No. *Just no.*"

I laugh. The sound is rusty, because I don't fucking do it very often, but still, I laugh.

"Kayden, quit causing shit and get home. If you don't, I'm calling Dragon."

"Fine," she mutters, and sadly takes her hand away. "See you around, Chains."

"Later," I respond. Then I watch as she walks away, my eyes glued to the way her ass sways in that barely there denim miniskirt. It bounces with each step and I swear a couple of times I could see the swell of her ass cheeks.

"She's underage," Nailer warns me.

I turn to look at him then and I can see the dislike on his face.

"How old?" I ask.

"Eighteen."

"I reckon that's legal."

"Not with her father being the President of the Savage Brothers it's not," he warns me and his words have the effect of wrapping my balls in cold ice.

Well fuck.

3

KAYDEN

The Den is definitely different in the daytime. It's empty. The seats are up on the tables, the worn, wood floors polished and ready for more traffic tonight. I've been here a few times, once or twice while it was open, but only because I was tagging along with my mom and/or my dad. Mom oversees the place. Dad gave it to her to manage years ago, before I was born. It doesn't seem like a place my mom would shine in, but then again, my mom shines anywhere.

It's also a place that has a special meaning to them. I don't know the whole story. But I've heard enough to know that this was the place that my dad decided to claim my mom as his old lady. My mom was a waitress here back then. In fact, the table that she waited on my dad and Uncle Crusher doesn't get used. It's sectioned off and Dad turned it into a booth. When he shows up that's where him and Mom stay. It's sweet. If you look at my dad, you wouldn't think he was sentimental in the least, but he is. He even bought the gas station where he first saw my mom. He always talks about how she was standing there, pumping gas. He says she was the prettiest damn thing that he had ever seen in his life and much too good for him. When he tells the story he's always staring straight at Mom. To this day, Mom blushes when she tells it too.

I might be young, but I know without a doubt that when I fall in love, that's exactly what I want. I refuse to settle for anything less. Mom always told me that when love is right, it creates miracles. She says that instead of it weathering with time, it becomes beautiful and passes in the blink of an eye.

I want that so damn bad.

Of course, between my dad, my brothers, and my numerous uncles that are strewn across several states... a man would have to be stupid to get within one foot of me.

For some reason, a picture of the man from last night sifts through my mind. I liked him. He's not my usual type. Not to be a bitch or anything, but I usually only look at men who have skin the color of my own. I mean my skin is on the lighter side because of mom. My hair is different than my girl Keanna's but still, everything about me screams BBC.

Big. Beautiful. Chocolate.

I'm never going to have small hips and I've definitely got junk in my trunk. I've been blessed with my mom's boobs and I like it that way. I've never doubted my worth as a woman or worried about what I looked like. I'm pretty and that's not being an egomaniac. I know I am. At the same time, my worth is not because I'm nice to look at. My mom has some horrific scars. She has a tattoo that covers most of them, but there are still some visible. That doesn't make my father look differently towards her. He still thinks she's the most beautiful woman in the world, and has constantly, despite her gaining baby weight and being what she calls 'fluffy'. He doesn't see the gray in her hair, or any of the things she bitches about. He sees bone deep beauty. I know, because he's told us often enough. It's because of this that I've always known beauty is on the inside. Some of the prettiest people I've ever seen are so ugly it hurts to look at them.

With parents giving lessons like that in your life, it's hard not to be grounded. I'm not saying life is perfect. Being who I am and an outlaw biker's kid can be hard. I've had foul words thrown at me, snickers behind my back, and numerous other things happen. For the most part, I've ignored it. Sometimes I would come home from school crying, but my parents never let the hurt fester. Dad always told me you learn to get tougher skin if you want to come out on top in this world and he's right.

Anyway, maybe because I've been burned in the past by boys who wanted to get in my pants because they wanted to brag they could fuck the biker princess, I've not dated a lot. When I did, I always looked for someone away from the club life. Someone who had no idea what this life is like.

Chains definitely doesn't fall in that category.

He has a lot of dark ink on him, hell I think he has more skulls on him than my uncle does—who is *named* Skull. He has muddy brown hair that's long and shaggy, but sexy as hell. And it was dark last night, but the light from the sign above the club shined down pretty bright and his blue eyes were clear, almost Prussian—which has always been my favorite color.

I laugh as I make my way to my office for the day. It doesn't matter what color home boy's eyes are, or what he looks like.

He's not for me.

There's a reason that at nineteen—well almost, I'll be nineteen soon—that I'm still a virgin. Boys might want to be seen with me and try to go there with me, but with watchdog brothers like mine, not to mention my dad and uncles... I'll be lucky if I don't die at eighty as a virgin.

Here lies Kayden Nicole West, she died from her va-jay-jay being overrun with cobwebs and smothering out all signs of life.

I sit down at my desk and drag out the ledger Mom has been keeping. She's slowly bringing me in as her replacement. I'm young, but I'm damn good at this kind of thing. I'm going to college to get my accounting degree and will have it done way before schedule because I've taken college classes in high school.

I have goals and I know exactly the life I want. I've always been like that and maybe that's why Dad and Mom trust me to take this step—even if they rather I did it while living at home.

Last night was only my fourth night in my own place, but I love it. It's just a small three-room apartment above the local flower shop downtown, but it feels like a mansion after living at home for so long with my two brothers and my parents.

I spend the next hour going over the books and highlighting some trouble spots. We could definitely turn more of a profit with a few changes. I want to make sure I talk to Mom about those when they make it back. Once I get all that done, I pack up. It wouldn't do for me to still be in the club by the time it opens. Nailer would probably come in and haul me out over his shoulder—which might hurt him. He's definitely on the slimmer side of life, even with muscles.

Nothing like the guy last night.

I sigh out from the memory. He was pretty, but I need to get him out of my mind. Chances are, I'll never see him again. I get my stuff together and walk to the door. Once I get it open, I can't stop the gasp that leaves my lips. Standing there against the wall in all his glory, is the guy from last night.

Chains.

He looks like he's just been standing there waiting for me. I do my best to ignore the trail of heat that runs through my system.

I fail... *Especially when he grins at me.*

Oh my. He has a beautiful grin. This time that trail of heat he causes shoots through me like a rocket.

Houston? I think we have a problem. Ovaries scheduled to burst in about T-minus ten seconds. 10, 9, 8...

4

CHAINS

I'm a fucking fool. She's much too young, her dad's the president of one of the biggest clubs around, and she's nothing but trouble. Still, after one look last night, I want more. I've been standing outside this damn office for twenty minutes—ever since I walked by and heard her humming happily through the door.

She gasps in surprise, shock clear to read on her features. She didn't expect to see me here. No, it's probably more than that. She didn't expect me to follow up on our meeting.

You ain't alone, baby. You ain't alone.

"Hi," she says, her lips moving into a grin, pleasure slowly replacing her astonishment.

"Hey."

"Were you waiting on me?"

"Probably," I respond with a shrug.

"You don't know?" she says with a small laugh.

"Not entirely. All I do know is that you are grade A trouble."

"You don't know me. How do you know I'm trouble?"

"Baby Girl, you reek of it."

"Maybe you shouldn't be here then," she says softly as she

walks toward me, stopping only when she's within touching distance. I curl my hand in a fist to keep from reaching out. I usually have really good control over my actions, but this girl definitely tests me.

"Oh, I *definitely* shouldn't be here."

"Then, why are you?" she asks, her head tilting to the side, watching me carefully with her dark eyes, the irises almost black. A man could get lost in those eyes.

Or found.

"You don't know me either."

"What's that mean?"

"Maybe I'm the kind of man who likes trouble."

"I think I like you, Chains, which sucks."

"Does it?" I say, not able to stop a surprised laugh. "I would have figured liking me was a real good thing, considering what I want to do to you."

"With a normal girl, yes. Not with me."

"Don't believe I'm following you, Kayden."

"I like you. It'd be a shame to get that pretty face of yours all messed up," she says.

That does make me laugh. I've just turned thirty and I don't think I've ever been referred to as *pretty* in my life.

"How about you let me worry about my face?"

"You're not from around here."

"What difference does that make?"

"The last guy to take an interest in me hopped in his truck and fled the state after one look at my Uncle Bull."

"I don't spook easily." I shrug, not concerned.

"That's what he said."

"How old was he?"

"He was twenty-two," she answers, frowning at me.

"Maybe your problem is that you were dealing with a boy and not a man."

"How old are you?" she asks.

"Old enough to know better and still too damn—"

"Young to care. Yeah, I've heard that before."

"How old are you, Kayden?"

"You know my name."

"The guy last night said it."

"And you heard him," she says with a nod.

"When things are important, I make sure to listen."

Her face goes soft and she likes what I said. I can tell. It's strange how she doesn't try and hide her thoughts from me. They seem to reflect right on her face. I've never known a woman like that before. I like it. With her, I'll never have to guess where I stand.

"I'll be nineteen next month," she responds and I do the quick math in my head.

"Almost eleven years difference."

"Eleven?" she asks, but I don't respond, there's no reason to. She frowns and then reaches over and touches the rocker panel on my cut. Her finger, which has a glossy red polish on it, traces my road name. "Am I too young for you, Chains?"

"I'll let you know," I tell her.

Slowly her gaze moves back up to lock on my eyes.

"What's next?" she asks, making me smile.

I capture her hand and bring it up to my mouth, pressing the scruff of my beard against her sweet little hand and kissing it while my gaze is still locked with hers. Beautiful white teeth come down and bite against her bottom lip and my cock presses against the zipper in my jeans.

Oh yeah. She's definitely going to be trouble. But, unfortunately for me, she's my favorite kind.

5

KAYDEN

That day at the Den with Chains excited me in ways I've never felt before. I thought it was the start of good things to come. I was looking forward to it. But after he kissed my hand he just left. That was three days ago and I've not heard or seen anything from him since. Maybe he gets his rocks off by playing games.

What the hell do I know?

I might be young, but I'm too old to play that kind of game.

"What's got you looking so pissed?"

I look up at Thomas and do my best to push everything else out of my head.

Including Chains.

"What are you talking about?"

"Kayden, you've barely been talking all night."

"You're being silly. You and Dom have been playing video games all night. There's been no reason for me to talk," I respond, hoping he buys it, but I doubt he will. Most people think Dom is the one who is most alert and never misses a thing, but I know that it's really Thomas. He's always wading in and calming the waters where Dad or Dom are concerned. Dad says he has Mom's peacemaking gene. That thought makes me smile. Still, the point is, Thomas is super sharp. I can never get anything past him.

"Calling bullshit on that one, Kayden."

"Whatever. Shouldn't you hurry? Dom is outside waiting," I remind him. "You know he gets impatient."

We're standing at my door. Thomas and Dom came over and had dinner with me, then they wasted hours playing video games. I was glad for the company, but I'm tired and more than a little sad over Chains—which is crazy. He teased me and then blew me off and it shouldn't make me sad. If that's his game, he's not worth my time. That doesn't mean it doesn't suck, though.

"We're not finished talking about this," Thomas warns. I frown, then let out a slow breath.

"Okay, but not tonight. I promise I'm fine. I'm just in a bit of a funk."

"About?"

"You wouldn't understand, Thomas."

"Try me."

"It's hard liking a guy and you think he feels the same, then he disappears. It just seems it always happens. I'm starting to think it's me."

"You're perfect, Sis."

"You'd think so, you're my big brother, you have to. But most guys—at least the ones I've met—don't want to fight an entire army to take me to the movies."

"Then they don't have any balls and you're better off without them," he grumbles, combing my hair away from my face.

"Probably, but that doesn't mean it's not lonely."

"I get that. It's hard when you have feelings for someone and they don't feel the same."

"That sounds like you're—"

"I'm not ready to talk about it right now either," he says, cutting me off.

"Soon then," I tell him.

"Soon."

"Bye Thomas," I tell him, reaching up to hug him.

"Lock your doors, Kay-Kay," he says, giving me a wink. I watch him walk away, going down the stairs that lead to the street.

With a sigh, I lock the door. I barely make it to my bedroom when I hear knocking. Obviously one of them forgot something. I look around and see Thomas's ball cap he was wearing and grab it. My brothers kill me. Apparently, I'll be picking up after them even now that I'm living on my own.

I make my way to the door, unlocking it, holding the ballcap out.

"Forgot something did you? I swear you and Dom—"

I stop talking when I see Chains standing there instead of my brother.

"Cute hat. Not my style though," he says and he's right. Chains has this thick mane of dark hair. It's high on his face, kind of haphazardly thrust back in a style that probably went out in the fifties, but it's updated somehow and looks lazy and sexy on him.

"What are you doing here?" I ask, ignoring the way my heart beats hard against my chest.

"Wanted to see you."

My eyes narrow at his reply.

"How did you know where I lived?"

"Was it supposed to be a secret?"

"Not exactly, but still—"

"Relax, Baby Girl. You're safe with me. Your father's men were talking about it at the clubhouse."

"You've been at my father's club?"

"You're a biker princess, you don't know the rules? I have to go by there when I come into town. Besides, Gunner arranged things so I could crash at The Den. I needed to show and introduce myself."

"Oh..."

"You going to let me in? Or are you going to wait around until your dates comes back?"

"Until... *My dates*?"

"It's your business, but I should warn you I'm not the kind of man to share my women."

"I don't... What are you talking about?"

"If I wade in there with you, then you're going to have to kick your boy toys to the curb."

I can't help but laugh.

"My *boy toys*?"

"You heard me."

"Let's see how it goes, then I'll talk to my... *boy toys.*"

"How it goes? You think you're going to try me out?" he grumbles.

"Well, if I decide to wade in there with you, I need to know you're worth it first," I respond, trying to keep from busting out in laughter.

"Trouble clean through. I should have known it. As long as you get that I don't share."

"I believe I get that."

"Good."

"So, you coming in or what?"

"I've changed my mind."

"What?" I ask, confused.

"I don't think I want to be that quick to come in and take the place of the men that came before me."

"The men? Listen, I think—"

"Saw them both leaving. Doesn't take a genius to figure out what you've been getting here and how you like it. That's why I'm telling you, I don't share what's mine."

"Wow. You got all that just from seeing Dom and Thomas leaving my place?"

"I've seen them at the club. I know they're prospects. If you're just trying to get back at Daddy, hey I'm cool. I can play that game. But, I don't share."

"Good to know," I mutter, rolling my eyes.

"You figure out if that's something you want to pursue. If so, meet me down at Freeman Park tomorrow about six."

"Freeman Park?"

"You know where it's at?"

"Well, yeah. I'm the one from here. I'm just surprised you do."

"Passed it just as I crossed the county line here. I figure there's not much that goes on that your dad won't hear about, but until we see what we have between us, there's no point in advertising it."

"You didn't strike me as the cautious type, Chains."

"All things in moderation. You think over what I told you. If you don't show, I'll have my answer."

"I don't think we—"

I want to explain about my brothers, but he steps into me, stopping me from talking. He curls his hand against the side of my neck, pulling me in deep. He stops when our lips are so close that when he speaks I feel his breath and a faint brush of his lips against mine.

"Before you make up your mind, I should get a shot at proving to you why you should show, right?" he whispers. I can't reply. I'm not sure I could speak if my life depended on it, but the point is moot because his lips slide against mine and I'm lost.

His lips are much softer than I would have imagined. His beard tickles my skin, but feels amazing at the same time. His tongue dances along my lip and I open my mouth, needing to give him entry—craving his kiss in a way that I've never wanted anything else before.

He growls into my mouth and I swallow that sound as our tongues wrap around each other, his asserting dominance and mine begging for more.

I'm not sure how long the kiss goes on, but when it stops my breath is coming in ragged gasps. I've been kissed before, but never like this.

"Tomorrow, Kayden," he promises, letting me go. He walks away; I'm stuck watching him.

He doesn't turn around and I can't turn away.

6

CHAINS

I need my fucking head examined. Kayden is obviously into playing games. She wants to tie her daddy up in knots and make him eat shit. I should have walked away the minute I saw them two kids go up to her apartment. I started to, but the strangest fucking thing happened.

I got jealous as hell.

I parked outside all fucking night, like some sort of damn creeper. I was so jealous that I couldn't see straight. I've never been jealous in my life. Fuck, I didn't even get jealous when I caught Angie sucking off another man and she had my ring on her damn finger.

"Normally when I show up on a date the guy doesn't look like he's ready to kill someone," Kayden says and I jerk my head up to look at her.

Fuck, she looks good.

She's wearing this skimpy as hell white dress with thin spaghetti straps. Her fucking tits are barely contained in it and the bottom of the dress falls on her thighs. If she was my woman, I'd chain her to the bed, spank her ass and demand that when she goes out in public she wear more clothes.

"You're looking good, Baby Girl."

"So are you," she smirks. Jesus, she's got so much fire in her that I have a feeling she could burn a man clear through.

"You remember when I said you were nothing but trouble?" I ask her.

"Yeah, I recall," she says with a sarcastic smirk.

"I'm thinking I was wrong."

"You were?"

"You're more dangerous than trouble. You're like a keg of dynamite ready to go off."

"Chains..."

"So much TNT packed in you a man will probably be sent off to meet his maker when you blow."

"Such romantic talk."

"That's who I am. Mr. Romance."

"Whatever," she says rolling her eyes. "Does this mean you're too scared to see where this goes?"

"This?"

"You and me, whatever this pull is between us. Listen, I may be young, but I'm not stupid. I know you feel the same chemistry. If you didn't, we wouldn't be doing this cat and mouse thing. So, don't try to play dumb with me. I don't have time for games."

"Are you always so direct?"

"Definitely."

"Good to know. So, you'll be kicking your boy toys to the side as long as I'm in the picture."

"If you would have stuck around last night, I would have told you about Dom and Thomas."

"I don't want to hear about them. Mostly the thought of them around you makes me want to fucking kill them."

"I don't think I'd like that," she says softly, her dark eyes going round in shock.

"I figured. So, for now, I just need to know you get that while you and I play our thing out, they are not in the picture."

"Play our thing out? That's just words to warm any girl's heart right there."

"It's not your heart I intend on warming, Kayden."

"You're right," she says, shaking her head. "You *are* Mr. Romance."

"I'm waiting on your answer," I tell her, tired of talking—at least about this.

"Answer?"

"Now who's playing games? It's simple. Are you kicking your boys to the side or not?"

"Not playing games, Chains. I'm just having trouble following the turns you take. But, to answer your question, Dom and Thomas won't be an issue while we... How did you say it? Play our thing out?"

"I can see you really liked how I said that."

"When something is important, you pay attention," she says, throwing my words back at me.

"Let's go," I tell her, standing up.

"Go? But I just got here. This is where you chose to meet, remember?"

"Now that the groundwork is settled, I want you on the back of my bike."

"Where are we going?"

"Next county over. Not about to invite your father's club's eyes today. What goes on between us, remains private—at least for now."

"Then, it's probably a bad time to tell you that my father has eyes everywhere, but especially in the next county over."

"Nothing but fucking trouble," I mutter, rubbing my beard. "Fuck it, we'll ride until I get tired. Whatever happens, happens."

"Whatever happens, happens," she says, her full lips stretching into a smile.

I put my hand on her back, barely stopping myself from letting it travel to her juicy ass. Then, I lead her back to my bike.

Messing with Kayden may wind up with me swinging at the end of a rope and not breathing. Dragon has a reputation and that's with men that aren't fucking his daughter. I can't talk myself out of this shit though. I want her.

And by God, I'm going to have her.

7

KAYDEN

Knowing you should walk away and walking away are two very different things. What Chains wants is totally clear. He's not trying to hide it. This is going to be all about sex and working whatever itch he has out of his system. That's not what I want, but at the same time, I'm pretty fucking tired of boys who run away when they find out who my dad is. Chains knows and instead of running, I'm pressed up against his body, riding on the back of his bike.

I thought I wanted anyone else but a man that lives the club life. I thought I had plans, but I lose sight of everything when Chains is near. Well, all except one thing.

Him.

I want more of him.

Which has to be the only reason I'm not walking away. I know the heartache he will leave me with is going to hurt like hell. I also know this could end very badly if my father finds out. But, it's like what my mom has always said.

"Some things are worth the pain."

Chains, I know, will be worth it. At least that's what I'm telling myself right now. I'll deal with the fallout later.

We ride for hours, and I'm not complaining. I'm a biker gal; I've always loved the freedom of being on the back of a bike. It's freaking awesome and the fact that Chains is in control and I'm on the back of *his* bike makes it even better. He finally pulls into a small dairy bar a few counties over. Dad still has some reach here, I'm sure he knows that. But, it's not Uncle Skull's territory so that's marginally better. I slide off his bike and he joins me. His hand immediately goes to the small of my back, his fingers stretching out over my skin, feeling as if they are burning through my dress, as he guides me to a picnic table.

"Burger and fries?" he asks taking off his sunglasses.

"Fries yes, skip the burger and give me a hotdog with chili instead." His lips twitch, but he doesn't respond, instead he just keeps staring at me. "What?" I finally ask.

"You need to try and not get into trouble while I'm over there."

"It will be a hardship, but I'll see what I can do," I mutter, making his lips twitch more.

Then, he surprises me, by leaning down and kissing me. Only it's not my lips he kisses. It's my cheek and as he slides his kiss against my skin, his fingers, tease the side of my neck.

"Nothing but trouble," he whispers, his breath softly hitting against the shell of my ear.

I don't know why that should make me feel so warm inside, but it definitely does.

8

CHAINS

"What happens if I don't want to go back?" Kayden asks and I smile. I definitely know where she's coming from.

We're in some small no name park. There are people milling about, but for the most part it's empty. Kayden is sitting on my jacket I spread out for her, and I'm lying on the grass, my head in her lap. I couldn't for the fucking life of me tell you how we ended up like this. Fuck, I don't even remember being comfortable enough with a woman to be like this. The closest I've been with a woman was sleeping after we fucked, or the actual fucking itself. Never have I just relaxed in the bright sun and talked...

Which is all we've done.

If I'm honest, that's all she's done. I've said very little, but I've heard her. I've listened to her talk about her parents and the love they share. I've memorized her laugh as she's talking about her brothers and the love she has for her uncles. Her uncle's names I recognize as members of the club and the men I've met don't jive with her sweet memories of them. The life she describes seems foreign to me. I've been in the club life off and on most of my adulthood. I've never truly been a member, choosing instead to ride nomad, drifting from one place to another. I've done this mostly because I never felt at home anywhere but in the service. I've always been the loner, the one who watched others from a distance. That's why it's so fucking strange that I can't seem to get any distance from Kayden. She's so fucking young, too damn young. I can't even remember being her age but, when she talks, she doesn't seem that young.

Christ, I'm in a hell of a lot of trouble.

"You're quiet. I'm here, talking your head off and I don't think you've said five words, Chains."

"I don't talk much, Kayden. That's who I am. I've never spoken much."

"Why's that?"

"I don't know. I guess I am of the mind if you don't have anything important to say there's no point in opening your mouth."

"What if I ask you questions? Will you answer?"

"Got nothing to hide, Baby Girl."

"Okay then, where are you from?"

"Been on the road so long, I think that qualifies as saying I'm from all over."

"Your eyes are closed and you can't see, but I'm giving you *that* look."

"What look?"

"The one that says you're being a big, fat jerk right now," she mumbles.

I look up at her then and her face is soft, her hair curtains her face and her lips call to me. *Plump, soft, and inviting...*

"If that's what that look says, you can give it to me anytime," I mutter, reaching up to hook my hand against the back of her neck and pull her mouth down as I lean up to capture it at the same time.

She immediately opens for me and I press my advantage by taking over her mouth, claiming it, because that's exactly what I want to do to this little firecracker who soothes something in me that I never realized needed soothing.

"You really know how to kiss, Chains," she gasps after we break apart and despite being turned on, being hard as a rock, I laugh.

I'm used to women who play games, who plot and think out their every move when it comes to men. Kayden doesn't even try. Maybe it's because she's so young, or maybe that's just who she is, but whatever the reason, I want more of her.

"Can I kiss you again?" she asks and... *fuck.*

"Come down here, Kayden."

"I..." she responds, unsure and looking around.

"Lay down here with me, Baby Girl," I tell her, taking her hand, while lifting my head and shifting so I can pull her beside me.

She curls into me immediately, fitting into me perfectly—fitting as if she was made to be there. I half roll so that I'm leaning over her, my thumb brushing against her soft skin.

"Hi," she whispers, suddenly sounding shy. This woman is a puzzle box that I will never solve. She's all fire and sass one moment and then the next she can appear so shy and sweet it makes me fucking dizzy.

"Like having you close," I murmur, touching our lips together as my hand moves down to her thigh.

"I like it too," she whispers. Her hand comes up and her fingers dive into my beard. I've noticed on the few times she has touched me, she always zeros in on the beard. I may never shave again because she seems fascinated by it. "What's your name? Your real name?" she asks.

"Dylan," I tell her, my fingers pushing up under her skirt.

"Dylan what?" she asks, her hand going to hold my wrist, keeping my hand from moving any farther.

"Dylan Allen," I respond, using my real name for the first time in more years than I want to count.

"That's a good name," she says those beautiful lips of hers smiling, swollen and glossy from our earlier kiss.

I should stop pressing my luck. I should pull my hand away, since she's holding onto it. But, I can see the hunger in her eyes. I have her in my arms and my hunger is even stronger than what I see in her. I can't make myself stop and I won't even try. I want Kayden. I want her and by God, I'm going to have her. I push my hand under her dress farther, even against her hold. My fingers move up her thighs, intent on only one thing... touching her the way I've been dreaming about since the moment I first laid eyes on her.

"Chains," she gasps, as the pads of my fingers rest against the heated material of her panties—the heated, *wet* material. She wants me. The proof is right here with my touch. Fuck, I can feel her pussy pulsing through the thin material. She's hungry for more.

Hungry for me.

"Kayden, give me your mouth," I growl, my control barely there, my voice hoarse with hunger.

"We can't do this," she says.

"We can and you better believe we will. I'm going to finger fuck you, Kayden. Right here. Right now. I'm going to make you come and swallow down your sweet cries, as you call out my name. Then, when I'm done, I'll lick my fingers clean, tasting every ounce of your sweet juices I can find."

"Someone might see," she says, trying to look around even now. But, she doesn't stop my fingers from stroking against her panties.

"I'll protect you. If they look over here, they might wonder what we're doing, they might even suspect, but they won't see you. I'll protect you, hide you from any eyes but my own, Baby Girl."

Slowly she takes her hand away, wraps it against the back of my neck and pulls my mouth even closer to hers.

There's my answer.

Why in the fuck does it feel like I just won the biggest prize of my life?

9

KAYDEN

I've lost my mind.

That's the only excuse I have. I've lost my mind. I'm lying on the ground in the middle of a public park, Chains is lying over me and his hand is cupping me through my panties.

Who is this person?

Correction... his fingers are wrapped around the elastic of my panties and...

"What... what are you doing?" I gasp.

"I'm taking your panties off," Chains mutters as he places kisses against my neck.

My body tenses and I want to call a stop to what he's doing, but the second his tongue flattens, licking along my pulse point of my neck, as his teeth drag against my skin, I tilt my head giving him better access. I can't think, I can only feel. I want more.

"Chains," I moan, my fingers pressing into his back.

"I got you, Baby Girl. I'm going to make you feel really good," he says and he already is. God, it feels so good that I can barely catch my breath. I lose sight of everything, lost in the hunger he's stirring in my body. Then, I hear the sound of my panties ripping. The fog in my mind immediately clears and I become aware of other things. Like the birds chirping around us—because we're outside. The sound of laughter, because in the distance there are people.

People.

"Stop, Chains. You have to stop," I hiss, trying to pull away from him. That's next to impossible, by the way, because he has me pinned down against the ground. He's not budging and there's no moving him. He's built, stacked, packed and *solid.* He makes me feel small and I've never felt small in my life.

"You say stop, but you're so fucking wet your panties are drenched, Kayden."

He mumbles the words against my skin and the graveled texture of his voice, the feel of his weight on me, the hunger radiating off of him... It all combines to send an all over body shiver careening through my body.

"We can't do this here—*Did you just rip off my panties?*" I cry as they are torn from my body. I know he did. I just can't *believe* he did it.

"They were in my way," he says and then, before I can berate him and tell him how crazy he is, two of his fingers slide between the lips of my pussy. "Fuck, you feel good," he growls, his mouth coming back to mine, his tongue thrusting inside, and taking me over at the exact time his fingers push inside.

I'm lost. There's too much pleasure involved, I can't fight it. I surrender to the moment, to his kiss, to his touch... *to him.*

"That's it, Baby. Just relax and let me make you feel good," he croons. His fingers press inside, not going deep, but enough that I feel full. His thumb sweeps across my aching clit. "That pussy of yours is so tight it's going to choke my dick, Kayden. You'll have to be a good little girl and suck on it and make it nice and wet before I fuck you. If you don't, it's liable to rip you apart."

"Oh God..."

"Are you going to be my good little girl, Kayden? Are you

going to take my cock into that sassy little mouth of yours and suck on it like it's your favorite candy?"

"Chains," I groan, my hips thrusting out, my pussy clenching down, as I try to ride his fingers.

"Answer me, Kayden," he warns, his voice stern.

I don't answer him at first, I can't. I can't think to form words, I can only feel. In retaliation, Chains pinches my clit, sending a sharp bolt of pain and pleasure through me.

"Yes," I cry and I can't be sure if I'm answering him, or if I'm just begging for more of what he just did.

"Yes, what?" he growls, biting into my neck.

"Yes, I'll suck you," I moan, "I'll do anything you want," I promise him and I'm not lying. If he just keeps doing what he's doing, I will give Chains anything he wants.

It's that freaking good.

"That's my good girl. You're going to give me anything I want, anytime I want, aren't you, Kayden?"

"I... yes... I'll give you anything you want, Chains," I whimper, feeling my orgasm coming, knowing it's going to be huge.

"Anywhere I want, right Kayden? You'll give me that sweet body of yours anytime and anywhere I demand it."

"Chains," I whimper, trying to focus and wondering why his words turn me on even more.

"Say it, Kayden. Admit you're going to be my very own fuck bunny, giving me that sweet pussy anytime I demand it, no matter where we're at."

"Oh God," I moan, my body pushing against him, bucking against his hand.

"You want to come, don't you, Baby Girl?"

"Fuck, yes," I growl, mindless now and frustrated because just when I'm about to go over the edge, he pulls his fingers away from my clit.

"Tell me what I want to hear," he says, and it sounds like he's laughing, enjoying my torture, but I can't be sure—I'm too far gone. "Tell me what I want to hear and I'll make you come so hard that you'll lose your mind," he promises. It's not an empty promise, because I'm already mindless with hunger and need.

"You're so damn cocky," I mumble, crying when again his fingers break their movement and pull away from my aching clit.

"Hard not to be, Baby Girl, when I got my fingers in your sweet pussy and you're needing me to fuck you hard. Now, quit challenging me and give me the words I want to hear so I can make you feel good."

"What words?" I ask, my mind blanking at the dark hunger I can see in his eyes. His lips are mere inches from mine. My heart is slamming against my chest and my breath is frozen. Something inside of me is telling me that this man will have the power to destroy me if I let him. He'll change me in ways that I can't even comprehend.

He smiles, and I think that smile is one I'd die to see every day.

"Admit you're mine, anytime, anywhere, Kayden. Admit it and I'll let you come."

"I don't belong to you, Chains," I respond. "I'm my own person."

"Your pussy is so wet it's drenching my hand, Kayden."

"I—"

"I'm finger fucking you in the middle of a park in broad daylight and even if it is a few counties away, it's still your father's fucking territory. I think you get what that means, having grown up in this world. So I'm putting my ass on the line for more of your sweetness. I want this vow from you. If I don't get it, then this goes no further."

I swallow, mesmerized by his eyes, moved by his words in ways I'm not ready to decipher.

"Anytime, anywhere you want me, Chains. I'm yours," I murmur, the words feeling immense, feeling like a promise I should fear and maybe I do, at least a little. But, not enough to stop this.

"That's my girl," he growls, then his mouth slams against mine, as his fingers dive back and forth against my clit and he pushes me over the edge.

I come.

I come hard, right there in the middle of the park, in broad daylight, with Chains swallowing my cries of pleasure.

And I'd do it all again...

10

CHAINS

"I still can't believe we did that," Kayden mutters, her head down. I put my finger under her chin and pull her face up so that she's looking at me.

"There wasn't a damn thing wrong with what we did," I grumble, not liking that she thinks there was.

"If my father catches wind of this, you'll think twice about that," she argues.

"I could give a fuck about your father, Kayden."

Her eyes go round at my words and from the look on her face, I can tell she doesn't like what I've said. I don't truly care. I'm not going to sugarcoat shit for her.

"Chains, you don't know my father..."

"I'm not a kid, I'm thirty, Baby Girl. I'm too damn old to be worrying about some girl's dad getting his balls in a knot because I'm fucking his daughter."

"Wow... that's really... sweet," she mutters.

"I'm not about roses and candlelight. Pretty sure you knew that before you agreed to meet with me."

She gets a funny look on her face and almost smiles.

"Figures," she mumbles.

"What's that?"

"Nothing. You just sounded like someone else I know," she says and I frown.

I put my hands on either side of her, effectively pinning her against the side of her car. I thrust my leg in between hers, letting my thigh push against her sweet pussy. I could almost swear I feel her heat, even through our clothes. When I finally get inside of her with my cock she's going to burn me alive.

"I don't think I like the idea of my woman thinking I remind her of another man, Kayden."

"I didn't... *your woman*?"

"That's what I said."

"I don't think I can qualify as your woman after one semi-date."

"Did I or didn't I have my hands down your pants?"

"I'm wearing a dress."

"Stop being a bitch. You gave yourself to me and until I let go of it, this is how we're going to play this game."

"This game? Maybe you should stop talking."

"Give me a kiss."

"Not sure I want to right now, just saying."

"Do it anyway," I tell her, fighting the urge to smile.

She leans in, tilting her head back and I meet her, kissing her hard and way too brief. After the taste of her I had earlier today, I want more—not tonight though. Tonight, I have to go to the Savage Clubhouse for a party. I was invited by Dancer, which is apparently the VP and the guy in charge while Dragon is out of town. I want to tell them I have more important shit to do, but that might lead to more questions than I want to deal with at the present time. Tomorrow, however, Kayden is mine.

"You could follow me home you know," Kayden says after the kiss is over. She wants more too.

"Got things I have to do tonight, but tomorrow you're mine. Don't make any plans."

"It's a good thing you kiss so great, or you seriously wouldn't be worth it, Chains."

"Get in the car and get home before I spank that sassy ass of yours," I tell her, holding the door open for her.

She climbs in the car and I close the door. I keep leaning on it, waiting. Once she starts the car and I still haven't moved, she rolls the window down.

"What?" she huffs, clearly annoyed with me.

"Click that seatbelt in place."

"You've got to be kidding me?"

I don't say anything, I don't feel I need to. Her eyes never leave mine and we stare at each other, a contest of wills. Finally, she sighs out loudly and buckles her seatbelt. I manage to hide my smile—but just barely. Once I step back, she starts backing out of the parking spot. I watch her go and then make my way to Betty.

It used to be that my bike was the only woman I wanted in my life.

Kayden may have completely changed that....

11

KAYDEN

"I can't believe your ass right now Kay-Kay!"

"Keanna, I'm *not* going to the party. I'm just driving up outside to pick Thomas up."

"You could have hooked a sister up," she complains.

"You know as well as I do that I'm not allowed at the parties. My dad would flip his shit if I was at one of those parties."

"Your dad would have flipped his shit if he knew you were in a public park with some man's fingers playing tease the taco, too. What good old Dad don't know, won't hurt him. Besides you could have kept your ass in the car. I would have got out and found your brother."

"Right, you would be looking for Dom. It's Thomas that needs the ride home."

"Potato, Poe-taught-toe," she mumbles and I laugh.

"Bitch, quit giving me trouble. I just called to tell you I won't be by tonight after all."

"It's all cool. I guess since I don't get to eye-fuck your brother—"

"God, that's so gross. Can you *not* use the word fuck in any form or fashion when it comes to my brother?"

"That's a physical impossibility," she says, her voice serious. I roll my eyes, because when Keanna speaks you either go along or ignore her.

There is no in between.

"Whatever, call me tomorrow."

"Will do. Later, girl."

"Later," I tell her and click my phone off, as I pull into the graveled parking area of my dad's club. Growing up, this place was a second home to me. It still is for family barbeques and things, but for the most part, I don't go around the club. I'm not stupid, I know what happens here, Mom too. They've been very open and I do have eyes. I also know my uncles and each of them love their wives as much as Dad does Mom. They keep their personal lives just that. Still, the unattached men and even some of the married ones that don't have the same relationships with their old ladies as my family does, have club whores and it gets wild. I never enjoyed that part of the club life. It's why I decided long ago never to date someone who was all about the club life. My family might not cheat on their old ladies, but I've seen enough cheating to know it happens and happens often in this world. That's probably unfair, because it happens outside this world too, it's just I see it more in the club. It's almost the norm...

I pick up my phone and text Thomas.

"I'm out here, Doofus."

"Be out in a second."

I read his response and sigh. I'm always going to spend my life being at my brothers beck and call. They are determined to drive me insane...

It's a good thing I love them.

There's definitely a party going on tonight. I imagine it's wilder inside, but it's starting to spill over out here. There are bonfires burning in old oil drums, that are dispersed along the side of the building. Men are drinking and playing cards on the tables and all of them have at least one woman—most of the time more—on their laps.

"And what are you doing here, pipsqueak?"

"Hey, Uncle Dancer," I laugh, jumping in surprise because he snuck up to my window and I didn't even see him.

"You're not supposed to be here. Your dad is going to cut off my balls and feed them to Leggo."

"Leggo is too finicky to eat your balls," I laugh. Leggo is a junkyard dog—meaning he has so many species in his pedigree you can't tell what breed he is. He looks evil, but he's always been a big puppy dog to me.

"You need to go, Kayden. You want to rebel, do it when your dad is here, or better yet, do it when Bull is on duty."

"Relax, I'm just here to pick up Thomas. You know he doesn't like this kind of thing."

"Yeah, crowds can be hard to take."

"You heading home to Aunt Carrie?"

"Yeah, had about all of this I can stand," he says. "I don't like being away from Carrie for too long. I tried to get Bull to handle the party tonight, but Skye has the graveyard shift this week at the hospital."

"If you didn't want a party, why have one? Aren't you supposed to be in charge while Dad is away?" I laugh.

"Freak, that fuck-head, planned it. Then, the asshole had to head out of town and stick me with it. It was supposed to be a get together because some men from the Ohio chapter came in and there's a nomad that Gunner sent this way in town."

"Nomad?" I ask, trying to sound bored, my heart beating hard in my chest.

"Yeah, he's been crashing at your mom's club. Surprised you haven't seen him while doing the books."

"Nailer makes sure I only get in there when the place is dead," I mutter. "You guys realize what a double standard it is that

Thomas and Dom get to live here and party and I can't even go inside the dang club," I add, annoyed.

"Take it up with your dad. I'm not touching that," he says, and honestly I knew that would be his answer.

"Whatever. Shouldn't you introduce me to this nomad? So I know if he's around the club when I'm there?"

"No need. Freak said the guy was planning on heading out at the end of the week."

"He is?" I ask, hoping I'm keeping the pain that information causes out of my voice.

"Far as I know, of course with the way our new girls are hanging on him over there, he may change his mind," Dancer laughs.

"Hey sis, sorry it took me a bit. I couldn't find my keys," Thomas says, walking around Uncle Dancer and going to the passenger side of my car.

"No, worries," I murmur, my heart feeling as if it's being squeezed so tight I can't breathe. I stare in the direction Uncle Dancer was looking, and over in the far corner I see Chains. He's talking to Nailer and Striker and there are two women hanging on each side of him. He has his arm around one and she's... *kissing the side of his neck.*

The image is burned in my mind, but I turn away from it, as Thomas climbs inside my car.

"Later, Kayden," Uncle Dancer says.

"Later," I respond, not looking at him. "You ready to go?" I ask Thomas, feeling sick.

"Yep. Can you take me to Mom and Dad's so I can crash?"

"Of course," I tell him, hoping I don't embarrass myself and cry.

"Then, let's get out of here," he says.

My hand shakes as I put the car in reverse.

"Drive safe, Kayden," Uncle Dancer calls loudly so that I hear him over the vehicle as I start backing.

My head jerks up and I do my best to muster a smile for him.

"I will," I tell him.

Against my will, my eyes go to Chains. My heart stutters in my chest when I see he's staring straight at me. Guess he heard Uncle Dancer call my name. I don't even think about it. I raise my hand and flip him off.

Chains can go fuck himself. I'm not about to let any man play me.

I should have stuck to my guns and never gotten involved with a biker. It sure as hell won't happen again.

No fucking way...

12

CHAINS

I never expected to find Striker here. He was brought back into service by the higher-up. They wanted him to oversee a special-ops mission that I took part in. He's standing with Nailer going on about some bullshit story that happened when I was stationed in Kabul and it brings back memories that I miss. I find myself relaxed and laughing for the first time tonight. I like the way of life in the club, because it reminds me of my military days. The sense of family, the camaraderie it all soothes something in me. It's why I seek out a club every now and then. Still, I've never felt I belonged full time in one—never even wanted that. I feel more relaxed at this club than I have at the others though, which is a welcomed change, especially since Kayden is here. After the taste I had of her today, there's no fucking way I want to leave any time soon. I had planned on leaving this week, but that's definitely not happening now. Christ, I'm thinking about her so much that I should be running in the opposite direction. The very last thing I need to do is get tangled all up over a woman.

"Let's get my boy some women," Striker yells. He's been drinking all night and feeling no fucking pain for sure.

"Nah, man. I'm good," I tell him, waving it off. I should probably try to lose myself in some easy pussy. Maybe if I fucked Kayden out of my mind I could move on. The thing is, I don't want it. I want her. I want her sweet moans in my ear. I want her body beneath me as I pound her hard. I want to feel her shatter and climax as I empty myself inside of her.

I want Kayden.

And, it might sound completely whacked, but I want her in a way that I know I can't substitute with any other woman.

I stifle a groan as the women come over, plastering themselves on each side. They're gorgeous, young and everything a man could want.

Any man but me.

I want to push them away, because honestly, it's a waste of their time. They're here to party and to fuck. It's what they want and I've always respected a woman who knew what she wanted and made no apologies for it. But the next woman to get my dick will be Kayden. Hell, these girls are half naked, toned bodies with soft honey hair and you'd think my dick would be hard as a rock, but he doesn't even move.

That's probably another sign that I'm in too deep with the biker princess. Where's my sense of self-preservation? That fight or flight instinct? Why the fuck am I not running away? Instead, I'm fantasizing about all the ways I'm going to fuck the president's daughter.

"What do you think, Chains?" Nailer asks.

"About what?" I ask completely lost in my thoughts.

"Hah! Having trouble concentrating with Trish's boobs pushed up in your face?"

"They're not pushed in his face," she says in a pouty little voice designed to make a man's dick stand up and weep.

My dick, the lazy fucker, continues to play dead.

At least I hope he's just playing.

"They could be though," she adds, looking up at me with her

big doe eyes.

"Mine could be wrapped around something else," her friend says and damn it, my dick still doesn't move.

"Now that sounds like a good way to spend the night," Striker says.

"You could join us," one of the girls says. Hell, I don't even know their names... I don't want to either.

"Sorry, girls. Unless he's changed a hell of a lot, Chains doesn't share his meals."

I grunt, because he's right, I don't.

"Oh, pooh. Maybe I can take Chains and Brandy could make you happy?" Trish, Tina or Tessa, says.

I can't remember her name. I just know, that for some reason, it feels like the damn walls are closing in on me. They're closing in and it's Kayden closing them. One of the girls moves her hand down to the button on my pants. I capture it in mine, applying more pressure than I should. I'm about to tell her to stop and for both of them to go tend to Striker when the Savage VP, Dancer, yells out, grabbing my attention.

"Drive safe, Kayden," he says, slapping his hand against her hood.

Kayden.

My gaze seeks her out. She looks up at me and I see the anger in her face, even from this distance. I also see one of those fucking prospects in her car. One of the same ones that practically spent the night in her house the other day. If she thinks she can give another man what I claimed as mine earlier today, then she's in for a hard fall. That's not about to happen. I won't let it.

I'm about to charge over there and tell her exactly that. I don't care that we're at her father's club and claiming her in front of them will get my ass kicked. I even take a step to do exactly that. Then, Kayden puts her hand outside her car window and flips me off.

Baby Girl just declared war and she doesn't even know it....

13

KAYDEN

"Where have you been?"

I stumble at my door when Chains steps out from the dark corner. Instantly, anger pushes through me, replacing the despair I was feeling just moments earlier.

"What the fuck are you doing here?" I growl, clutching my key in my hand.

"Answer me, Kayden. Where have you been?"

"That is none of your business. Shouldn't you be out fucking your Twinkies?"

"Twinkies?"

"Club whores."

"Did you fuck him?" he asks, not bothering to answer me.

"Get the hell out of here, Chains."

"I'm not going anywhere. You need to answer the damn question."

"I don't know where you get off," I tell him, deciding enough is enough.

"That's easy," he smirks. "I'm getting off in you."

"The fuck you are. That's not happening. Not now."

"I like when you show me what a dirty mouth you have, Kayden. It makes me want to put my dick in it and wash it clean."

"I...Oh my God! I get it now. You're certifiably insane. Yes! I fucked him," I lie. "I fucked him twice as hard for the two bitches you had hanging all over you. I fucked him and it was so good. If he knew you were the one that got me all worked up, he'd probably send you a thank you card. Trouble is, I'm worn out now, so you'll just have to leave. I'm afraid after the night I had, I don't have time to give you a go. Check back tomorrow—or better yet, how about *never*?"

"You need to be careful, Kayden. I'm not some little boy you can play with," he says and I can hear the anger in his voice, I just don't give a damn.

"Ask me if I care, Chains? I'm tired of your controlling attitude and your ego the size of damn Texas. I want you to leave. In fact, I'm warning you, you better leave."

"I don't want to."

"I don't care what you want. You need to leave, if you don't—"

"You'll what?" he says, his voice a mocking laugh that fills me with anger, but also sends a cold chill down my spine.

"Just leave, Chains. Whatever fun you had, it is over."

"I seem to recall you having fun, too. Are you forgetting that Kayden?"

"I'm forgetting nothing. Including the way you were getting ready to fuck two women when I last saw you."

"So you thought, what? You'd just give away what you gave to me? Let some other man put his hands on you to get even with me?"

"This might surprise you, Chains, but I didn't think of you at all when I had his hands on me."

I'm lying through my teeth. I'm not about to admit that Thomas is my brother, however. I am not going to admit how much he hurt me either. I have a lot of my father in me and when I'm done, I'm done. Chains won't get the opportunity to hurt me again.

"You're playing a dangerous game, Kayden."

"That's the difference between you and me," I snarl. "I'm not into playing games. You, on the other hand seem to enjoy cornering the market on that shit. Still, just so it's crystal clear and you understand, I'll spell it out for you."

"Do that," he says, the same dark look on his face, a smile that isn't quite there, just a ghost of it. It's also not cocky now, not at all. It's almost... *evil.*

I ignore the fear that skates down my back. I just need rid of Chains. He can go back to his whores. He'll leave at the end of the week like Uncle Dancer said and I'll cry him out of my system. And this time, I'll make sure I never forget the million reasons why I don't want to be with a man that lives the club life.

"What we had or played around with, however you want to explain it, is over. It's done. I don't have a place for you in my world. So, go back to your whores and your world. With any luck, you and I will never have to see each other again."

"That's not the way this is going to go, Baby Girl."

"It is the way it's going to go. You don't have a choice."

He shakes his head back and forth very slowly, his eyes trained on me, his face almost cold.

"Leave Chains, or I'll make sure you leave."

"How do you plan on doing that?" he asks, his lips spreading into a smile that shows amusement and that just pisses me off. I've had it. I'm not here for this asshole to make fun of me. It's bad enough that I let him hurt me. I refuse to let him mock me.

I pick up the phone and dial the number that I know by heart. Chains doesn't make a move to stop me. I don't know why, but part of me was hoping he would. Maybe, because I know this is the one thing that will end any association I have with Chains.

That's what I want, it has to be. I can't have someone who hurts me so carelessly. I don't want a player in my life. I cared about Chains and it's clear that those feelings aren't returned—not even a little bit. That's a hard pill to swallow, but I do it just the same.

"Kayden? You okay?"

"Uncle Dancer?" I respond and I can't stop the hurt from coming through my voice. I can even hear my tears. I haven't got to cry yet, not with spending time with Thomas. Now, knowing that I'm going to make it impossible to ever see Chains again, those emotions are trying to get the better of me. I don't give into it, but it's definitely hard to hold back the emotion.

"What's wrong, Kayden?" Uncle Dancer asks, instantly worried.

"Chains is here."

"Chains? The nomad?" Dancer asks.

"He's trying to get in my apartment, Uncle Dancer. Can you send Thomas and some of the others to make sure he leaves?"

"Motherfucker! Keep your doors locked. Do not let that asshole inside your apartment. I'll be right there," he growls, hanging up. I click off the phone and look at Chains in triumph —even if it is hollow.

"That was a mistake, Kayden," he says, somber, all signs of cockiness gone from his face.

"The way I figure it," I tell him, each word feeling as if they are heavy weights. "You have about twenty minutes, thirty tops before my uncle and the rest of the club get here. You need to get on your bike and get the hell out of town, Chains. It's over."

"Right," he says, pushing himself away from the wall.

I wait for him to leave. I'm not prepared for the way he stops right in front of me, pushing into my personal space.

"I—"

I break off, unable to say anything when his hand clamps around my wrist so tight that it's physically painful.

"Looks like we're going to do this the hard way, Kayden," he says and before I know what he's doing, and can do anything to stop him, he lifts my body up and throws me over his shoulder.

I scream out, feeling as if I'm falling. I scramble to try and get out of his hold and find my balance.

"What are you doing?"

"If I'm leaving town, Kayden. Then, so are you. I told you before and you should have listened."

"Listened to what? Oh my God! You're crazy. You need to let me go and get out of here. Don't you realize what my family will do to you?"

"You vowed that you were mine, anytime and anywhere I wanted you. I'm not going away just because you got your ass all twisted up thinking I was fucking other women. I'm not even going away knowing you gave what was mine away to another man. But, you'll damn well be punished for that and when I'm done with you—"

"Chains, stop this. You're talking crazy. There's still time. Put me down and head out of here. I'll tell my uncle that I was just pissed at you. I'll cover so they don't chase—"

"I'm leaving, but you're coming with me and when I'm done with you Kayden, you'll be too damn tired to even look at another man."

"Chains—"

"And you sure as hell won't be able to give him what belongs to me," he growls.

I've never had a panic attack, but I'm pretty sure when Chains puts me on the ground, I go into one. My body is shaking from the anger on Chains face—anger that he somehow managed to hide before. His hand thrusts down into my pants pocket. He takes out my car keys and I watch as he hits the button to unlock my doors. Next, he takes my phone which I somehow, miraculously, manage to still have in my hands and he tosses it on the concrete. My eyes go to my precious cellphone with a now completely shattered screen. When I tear my eyes away to look back at Chains, he's smiling. He's smiling and he's still angry.

That's when I one hundred percent, unequivocally, know that I'm in trouble.

Oh shit.

14

CHAINS

"You need to stop this craziness," Kayden says for maybe the hundredth time. You would think the fact that I've been ignoring her would clue her in. I'll say this for my girl, she's persistent if nothing else. "Will you talk to me?!?!" she huffs, when I fail to respond.

"Don't have much to say," I tell her and that's the damned truth. Right now I'm concentrating on putting as much asphalt down between us and her dad's club as I can. It's taking me a ridiculous amount of time, because I'm taking only backroads and sometimes I end up going in circles. It would be much quicker to just drive directly there, but I'm not leaving them an easy trail. I'm not stupid, I know eventually they're going to catch up to me, but I'm hoping I can gain enough time between then and now.

I want more of Kayden, and I'm going to get it. Hopefully, by the time we've had our fun together she can soothe Daddy's feelings and I'll be long gone. It's a shit plan, but it's all I have. I can't make myself walk away from her. She's like a fire in my blood. That means taking Kayden and playing it this way will most likely drag both of us down.

I've even resigned myself to the knowledge that I most likely won't survive this shit. That's a pretty fucked up way for me to go—taken out because I'm tangled up over a woman. I guess if a man has to go, there's worse ways of dying than between the legs of one as sweet as Kayden.

And, I am going to get between her legs.

There's no stopping that.

"You're going to get yourself killed, Chains."

"Probably," I admit, seeing no reason to lie about it.

"You're insane. That's the only possible explanation. How did I not see that sooner?"

"You're cute as hell when you're upset, Baby Girl, but it's going to be a long ass trip if you insist on keeping this shit up the whole time."

"This...*shit*?"

"That's what I said."

"Do you have any idea what you've done?"

I glance at her, giving her an are-you-fucking-serious look, because I think it's pretty clear what I've done.

"This isn't a game, Chains. I don't know what's wrong in your head, what makes you think that you can get away with this, but my dad will kill you."

"He can try."

"He won't just try, you idiot," she snaps. "He will! You have to stop this. Pull over at the next gas station and I can call Thomas to come and get me. I'll tell them I was joking that I have no idea where you are. I'll cover for you."

"Nice try, Baby, but you're not escaping your punishment."

"My punishment!?!?!" she shrieks. "I'm trying to save your life, you dumbass."

"Careful, Kayden. It almost sounds like you care."

"I do! I don't want my dad to kill you, Chains. You have to stop this before it's too late."

"It already is. I left Betty back at your apartment. They're not going to buy the idea that you don't know where I'm at. So, why not just sit back and enjoy the ride at this point?"

"Betty? You left one of your club whores at my apartment?"

I frown, and then laugh because I can't stop myself.

"I don't see anything about this funny, Chains."

"You wouldn't, you're too busy being a pain in my ass."

"Fine, let Dad kill you. Maybe one of your whores can cut off your dick and bronze it to remember you by."

Jesus, she comes up with some of the craziest shit.

"It's good you think my dick is so impressive it should be bronzed after I die."

"I wouldn't know. I just figured that'd be what *Betty* would want to keep."

"I doubt Betty cares since she's my bike."

"You named your bike... Betty?"

"Yep."

"Why?"

"Because she's mean and temperamental, just like a woman."

"Your judgement of women is so flattering," she mutters.

"It's just the simple truth," I counter.

"Probably so, around you," she mumbles.

"What's that mean?"

"It means women tend to get mean when you play with their emotions."

"How in the fuck did I do that? You're the one who let that fucking prospect between your legs after promising me that your body was mine. You're lucky I didn't fuck you right in front of your dad's entire club and prove who owns you."

"First of all, no one *owns* me—"

"I do."

"Second of all," she says, acting like I didn't even speak and giving me a pissed off look that makes me want to kiss the hell out of her. "If you tried to touch me at the club, my uncles and cousins would have taken you down so quick, you wouldn't have known what hit you. And, third—"

"You have an awful lot of confidence in your daddy's men," I mumble, wondering why that should piss me off—just knowing it does.

"And third, if you'd tried to fuck me I would have cut your dick off and fed it to the Twinkies hanging all over you."

"My girl can be vicious," I respond, shaking my head as I merge into the other lane to pass a log truck on my right.

"I'm not being vicious," she says with a shrug, as if she's not pissed right now, even though I know she would love to claw my eyes out. She looks at me, I can see her through my peripheral vision when she smiles. It's not a warm smile, it's a spirited smile that's full of challenge and makes me want to fuck her until we both can't move. "I'd just be giving them what they were begging for when they were crawling all over you like fleas."

"Fleas?" I laugh.

"That's what happens when you lay with dogs, or in this case bitches in heat."

She turns away from me then, choosing to look out the passenger window and dismissing me.

"I didn't sleep with them, Kayden."

"Not my business who you sleep with, Chains."

"You seem pretty pissed for someone who doesn't care."

"Nope. Although, I am sad for you."

"Sad?" I ask, completely amused and wondering what turn her sassy mouth is going to take now. I swear this woman keeps me guessing and I have to admit that I love every fucking minute of it.

"Yeah, because if you're telling the truth and didn't fuck them, which you're probably not—"

"Kayden, damn it—"

"It's bad because it would have been the last fuck you'll ever get. Soon, my dad will catch up with you, and when he does, he'll kill you and take his time doing it," she says, sounding like the thought actually cheers her up.

"Your father may actually succeed in killing me, Baby Girl."

"Yeah, he will," she says, still looking out the window.

"But he'll do it with the cum from your juicy cunt coating my cock."

She practically jumps in her seat and she turns to look at me then, her mouth open in shock. I give her a wink and then turn my attention back to the road. I know where I'm headed and with any luck, none of the Savage Brothers will be able to find us for a long damn time.

15

KAYDEN

"Thank God. I need to stretch my legs," I moan when Chains finally pulls into a gas station. We've been driving for hours. Dad insisted I get a car cheap on gas, he said it was economical. I say it's because he didn't want me speeding. Still, I didn't mind, but the fact I had just filled my tank up, then was kidnapped and forced to ride for hours upon hours without stopping, sucks balls.

"Sorry, Baby Girl, that's not happening," he says and before I know what he's doing, he grabs my hand, slaps a handcuff on my wrist and locks the other one to the steering wheel.

"You have got to be kidding me!" I growl, yanking my hand back and forth to try and get free.

"Can't have you trying to escape, now can I?" he says with a wink.

I'm really beginning to despise the way he winks.

"Chains, you let me out of this car right now or I'll scream so loud that the cops will come running to take you down."

"You'd really do that, wouldn't you?" he asks, studying me closely.

"In a fucking heartbeat," I promise him.

"I had hoped to gag you with my cock, but someone has to pump the gas. This will have to work in a pinch," he says. He takes out...

"Oh my God! Is that my panties?"

"Yeah. I hate to do it, but if you're going to scream, I don't really have a choice. I'll have to cuff your other hand too. You're really making this so much harder than it needs to be, Kayden."

"You are literally insane," I whisper pushing away from him—not that I can get far, seeing as how I'm cuffed to the steering wheel.

"If I am, it's because you made me this way. A man doesn't like claiming a woman and then watching her give it away to someone else. I warned you from the beginning, I don't share Kayden. You should have listened."

"You put that in my mouth and you won't have to worry about my father, Chains. I'll kill you."

"It's okay, Baby. I've cum all over these more than a few times. You'll like them in your mouth," he smirks, holding my panties between his fingers and waving them.

I'm equal parts outraged, freaked out and turned on and I can't figure out why that last one is even happening.

"Absolutely not. You are not putting that in my mouth."

"You're not leaving me much choice, Kayden. I have to pump the gas and take a piss. I can't do that if I'm worried you're going to make a commotion."

"You get to piss and I don't?"

"We'll be somewhere soon where you can. But if you're going to insist, I'll take you to the men's room when I'm done."

"Gee, you're all heart," I mutter, starting to form a plan in my mind.

"All heart and a big dick," he says with a grin. "Now, are we going to do this the easy way, or the hard?"

"If I'm good, do you promise to take me to the restroom when you're done?"

"Yep."

"Fine, then I'll make sure I'm good."

"Can I trust you?"

"On this, only because if I don't pee I'll end up ruining my car seat. Not that you would care, but I happen to like my car."

"Fair enough. Although I'm a little sad I don't get to stuff these babies in that delectable mouth of yours."

"If you so much as tried, I would have clamped down on your jugular and yanked it out with my teeth," I warn him, not completely joking.

"You're going to have to get over this aversion you have of things being stuffed in your mouth, Kayden. It might cause problems in our future relationship."

"I'd worry about that if you weren't a walking dead man," I mumble refusing to think he looks sexy right now with that cocky grin and those dark eyes of his glinting with victory.

"So much confidence in your father. Just think what could happen if you have that much confidence in me, Baby Girl," he says softly, the playfulness gone from his face so abruptly that I have to blink to make sure I'm not seeing things. Then, his thumb caresses against my lips as if he's carefully thinking something over, his gaze not truly focusing on me, instead cloudy and distant in thought. He kisses me. Barely more than a lip touch, a whispered breath against my skin and then he's gone, slamming the car door shut.

I have a feeling I've hurt him somehow and I have no idea how. I shrug it off because obviously, I'm starting to suffer from some sort of Stockholm syndrome or some shit. I remind myself he was the one with Twinkies draped all over him after blowing me off for the evening. The memory of that is *painfully* easy to pull up. Then, I recall how he not only kidnapped me, but destroyed my cellphone and threatened to stuff used panties in my mouth. This isn't some great romance, where the guy is just misunderstood. He's obviously unhinged, even if Keanna would approve that he's hot as hell.

With that in mind, I look to make sure Chains is nowhere around. My eyes track him through the windows of the store and see him going into the restroom. Quickly I stretch my body and reach over to the passenger side. I shift so I can reach under the seat, wincing at the pain it causes when the metal of the cuff presses into my wrist. I fumble for a little while, searching aimlessly, the tips of my fingers finally finding what I need. I'm so excited a startled squeal leaves my lips and then I quickly look over my shoulder, half expecting to see Chains there.

I breathe a sigh of relief when I don't.

"Thank God," I mutter. Then, focus all of my attention on capturing the Tracfone that Dad makes me and my brothers carry in our vehicles at all time. I thought it was annoying, but now I'm starting to see his reasoning. I grab it quickly. It's old school, hopefully useless for anything but emergency calls. I flip —*yes flip*—it open and dial the number Dad made us memorize before we were barely old enough to make complete sentences.

"Kayden! Where in the fuck are you?"

My eyes close and I smile, instantly feeling better about anything.

"I'm okay, Dad."

"Then why did Dance tell me you've been kidnapped? Why in the fuck can none of my men find you and why am I heading back from Tennessee with half an army with me?"

"Is that my baby? Oh God, Dragon, is that Kayden?" Mom cries.

"I'm okay, Dad. Chains... he won't hurt me. He's just... he's not taking our breakup well."

"Breakup? What in the fuck? Did that bastard touch you, Kayden? What in the hell do you mean breakup? Dance said he just came into town."

"He did... we had a date or two... well one and a half really."

"Kayden—"

"Dad, I don't have long to talk. Chains will be back out in a minute and I need to hide the phone. We're at a gas station, it's a Double Kwik on the Kentucky, Virginia state line. We passed a road sign a bit ago that had Wise, Virginia on it, but I'm not sure how many miles away it said it was. I don't know where we're going, but I'll try and check in again soon. But, the main thing is I'm fine. Chains won't hurt me."

"I'm going to fucking kill him," Dad yells. "I'll rip him apart from the inside out with my bare motherfucking hands!"

"Let me talk to my baby," Mom cries and there's scuffling over the phone, and I know Dad doesn't want to give up the phone, but like she always does... *Mom wins.*

"Kayden baby, are you okay?"

"I'm fine, Mom. I swear. I got to go, though. Just calm Daddy down. I'm fine and Chains won't hurt me. He's just upset I broke up with him after seeing him with the Twinkies at the club."

"Broke up with him? Twinkies? Kayden what exactly is going on here?"

I look over my shoulder and see Chains coming out the door. I turn so all he can see is my back and I hold my head down, letting my hair cover the phone.

"I got to go, Mom. He's coming back. I'll check in soon. I love you, tell Dad I love him, too."

I click the phone off and all but throw it under the passenger seat, turning around just in time for Chains to show up at the door. He watches me closely for a minute, as if trying to figure out what I've been doing—or maybe reading the guilt on my face.

The problem is I'm not sure what I feel guilty about...

"Everything okay?" he asks, opening the door.

I move my hand back and forth, looking pointedly at the handcuff.

"Depends on what you mean by okay," I mumble and he grins.

I ignore that his grin makes my pussy clench with want. I don't know why I'm still attracted to him. He clearly has some kind of undefined mental damage. Hell, maybe I do too, because I can't deny he's sexy or that part of me would really like it if he kissed me again...

Shit...

16

DRAGON

"Tell me you managed to trace that fucking call."

"Dragon—"

"Freak, if you didn't fucking get me some kind of lead on my daughter, you better be hiding when I get there."

"Damn it, Dragon."

"Don't you Dragon me. How you fucking assholes could let my girl get fucking kidnapped while I was out of town is beyond me. I told you dick-weeds to keep her under surveillance when you told me she moved out!"

"She'd been at your place with Thomas. The minute she left, he called Dom to go make sure she was secure."

"Where in the fuck was Dom?"

"I don't think you'll like that answer. He called Raze, but by the time Raze got there..."

"Christ. Where in the hell was Bull and Dancer during this shit? I didn't leave the club with wet behind the ear kids, even if some of those kids are my own blood. Where in the fuck were you guys?"

"It was a party. Bull was home because Skye was working graveyard and he needed to be there for Gypsy. Dance stayed at the party, but left before shit got too wild. He didn't want Carrie giving him shit. She's already giving him hell over Hawk and him fighting about the club."

"Jesus. Years ago I thought about striking a match to the whole fucking clubhouse and walking away. Now, here I am, years later, wishing I had fucking done that very thing. You get Gunner on the phone and you conference me in. This is his boy. Kayden told me they were headed toward Wise, Virginia. I want to know who in the fuck this Chains knows in that area and where he might be heading and I want to know it like two minutes ago. You feelin' me?"

"I'll call right back," Freak says and disconnects.

I hang up the phone still full of anger.

"DRAGON," Nicole whispers, her voice is full of fear and sadness. It's a sound that I swore to myself would never come out of her mouth again. I've busted my balls since the day she took my sorry ass back to make her nothing but happy. I'd succeeded until today.

"I don't know anything new, Nicole. I've got Freak working and the entire club is out looking."

"If something happens to her, I'll never forgive myself."

"Nothing's going to happen to her, Mama. I won't let it," I promise her.

I just hope it's a promise I can keep.

17

CHAINS

My sweet Kayden is up to something. I have no idea what it is, but she's been acting strange ever since I stopped at the gas station. She's probably plotting a way to get free. With any luck, I'll work this anger out of her the right way and leaving will be the last thing on her mind.

That's the plan at least.

I haven't slept. Instead, I drove through the night. I'm going to have to stop soon, though. Kayden hasn't said anything, but I know she needs a break. I'm feeling a little guilty for taking her, but not enough to stop now. Kayden has been catered to her whole life. I can tell.

If she thinks she can play me like she has the other men in her life, she needs to think again. Taming Kayden is definitely not going to be easy, but then, if she wasn't a challenge, I probably wouldn't be under her spell like I am.

I take the next exit off the road. I've stayed on the interstate most of the time, but the last little bit, I've been driving backroads. If Dragon's men are close behind me, they won't be expecting me to take the backroads—at least that's what I'm banking on.

"Where are we going?"

"I'm tired. I can't keep driving, I don't want to risk getting you hurt."

"It's the middle of the day."

"And I haven't slept in over twenty-four hours."

"I thought bikers were tough as nails," she mocks.

"If we were on my bike, I'd be good. But, in a cage, with you here smelling so fucking good, I'm staying hard as a rock and I need a bed."

Her eyes dilate and her mouth opens into a perfect 'o'. I grin.

"I'm not sleeping with you," she huffs. I keep grinning. "I'm serious, Chains. We are not having sex."

"You can't deny you want me, Kayden. Or did you forget how good it was when I got you off?"

"It was good. Then you played games."

"The hell I did. A man doesn't play games. I don't know what you're used to, but I'm nothing like those boys you've been hanging around with. I *know* what to do with a woman."

"Yeah, that much was clear when I showed up at the club and you had Twinkies hanging all over your ass."

"You can't complain about that, Kayden. You're the one that was there to pick up another man. Never mind that you were doing it not hours after riding the fuck out of my hand."

"I was there to pick up Thomas. He needed a ride."

"Tell me another one, Baby Girl, tell me another one."

"I'm serious. They're doing something to his bike and Dom was busy, he needed a ride."

"Did you give him one? I mean I worked you up for it right?"

"You're disgusting," she mumbles, curling her nose. "You need to stop at the store before we find a hotel."

"Don't have time for that."

"Then make time," she orders.

"No."

"Listen, Chains, I don't know what kind of girls you're used to—"

"None. I make sure they're *women,*" I tell her, then mutter under my breath, "That could be where I went wrong here."

"Fuck you," she says, telling me that there are no problems whatsoever with her hearing. "I think you get my dad is black and my mom is white, right?"

"What are you bitching about now?"

"All this fabulousness," she says waving at her dark hair that falls in gorgeous curls all around her head.

"It is pretty fucking fabulous," I admit, wanting it in my hands as I fuck her hard from behind.

"Well it doesn't just happen without work. I need coconut oil."

"Coconut oil?"

"I usually special-order stuff, but I doubt you're going to find anything like what I want. So, this will work in a pinch."

"You're sending me to the store to get shit for your hair?"

"You don't like it, you can let me out and I'll call someone to come get me *and* get shit for my hair."

"Jesus, how did I not know how fucking high maintenance you were?"

"Jesus, how did I not know how psychotic you were?" she mimics and turns back around to look out the window.

She's not looking so I figure it's safe to smile then...

Damn it... I really like her.

18

KAYDEN

"What are you doing?"

I look up at Chains in surprise. He's been pretty quiet since we got here. I am completely worn out, despite it being daylight outside. I'm not sure I can handle talking to him right now. I have too much going through my mind and I don't know what to think about him. The fact that he's kidnapped me and insists on dragging me with him—apparently through the entire state of Virginia—leaves me wondering if he's Coo-coo for Cocoa Puffs.

"I would have thought you could tell, but I'm braiding my hair."

"I can tell what you're doing, I just don't know why. I thought you were going to sleep."

"I am after I get my hair under control."

"Let me do it," he mutters, getting on the bed beside me.

"*You* know how to braid hair? You do know my hair is different, right?"

"I can do it."

"Why do I find this so hard to believe?"

"I know how to do a lot of things that would probably surprise you. Now quit being a pain in my ass and turn around."

I look up at him skeptically, but when he shows no sign of relenting, I let out an annoyed breath and turn around.

"If you fuck up my hair, Chains, my dad will be the least of your worries," I mumble, crossing my legs and sitting on the bed, my back to him.

He shifts and then his long legs stretch out on either side of me, his fingers moving to my hair. Suddenly it feels like I'm surrounded by him and this awareness moves through me. My hands tremble and I wring them together, hiding them in my lap, ignoring the dampness gathering between my legs. I shouldn't want Chains, especially now. I shouldn't be turned on by him because there's a chance—a very big chance—that he's crazy. My father will kill him if I don't stop it, too. My dad is explosive on a good day. He'll be ballistic by the time I make it back to him—that's if he doesn't find us first and for Chains' sake... I hope he doesn't.

My eyes close as I enjoy the feel of his fingers in my hair. I have to admit that I don't care what he does to my hair at this point, I just love the feel of his hands... I'm in deep shit when it comes to this man.

"You've gone quiet," Chains says and I keep my eyes closed, but his voice, soft yet graveled, just adds to the hunger that is building inside of me.

"I was wondering where you learned to braid hair," I lie.

"I have three younger sisters. Mom worked two jobs. It was sink or swim. I may not do this shit perfectly, but I'm decent at it, so relax."

"If I get any more relaxed, I'll be snoring," I joke.

"I wouldn't mind it."

"How can you be so sweet one minute and infuriating the next?" I mumble, completely confused by him.

"I was wondering the same about you."

"It's a gift I guess," I respond, making him laugh.

"Chains, you need to stop this. It's not too late. Let me go home and calm my father down."

"I'm not letting you go, Kayden. I..."

"What?" I ask, when he doesn't finish.

"Part of me almost wishes that I could, but the simple fact is, I'm not ready to let you go and I think—despite your arguing—you don't want me to let you go either."

I swallow nervously, because he's not wrong. I don't tell him that, however. I can't. I'm not lying about my father. This has disaster written everywhere I look.

"You have to know this is impossible," I murmur instead, looking down at my hands which are still folded together.

"Maybe, maybe not. How can we know if we don't give it a shot?"

"Funny you mentioned the word shot, because my dad—"

"Kayden? How about for at least the next two days you do your best not to mention or talk about your dad and we just spend time together."

"Why? What's the point, Chains? You're a drifter who won't even join a club because you refuse to put down roots. I'm most likely never leaving Kentucky. I love living there and being close to my family. You're the type of man a girl tastes once and lets go. Which is fine, but I'm the kind of girl who likes to taste the same thing over and over for the rest of her life."

"Are you comparing me to food?"

"You know what I'm saying. Quit being an asshole," I mumble, rolling my eyes.

"Finished with your hair," he says, surprising me.

I slide off the bed and walk into the small bathroom. The braids are a little wonky here and there, and not at all what I wanted, but it's not bad—just different, and the fact he did it surprises the hell out of me. When I come back in, he's lying on the bed, the covers pulled down and smiling up at me.

"Comfortable," I ask, feeling anything but.

"Admit it, you're surprised."

"Whatever," I return, going to the second bed in the room.

"You can stop right there," Chains says.

"What?" I ask, confused.

"You're sleeping with me."

My eyebrows raise and motion no with my head. "You're crazy," I laugh. "There's no way in hell I'm sleeping with you."

He gets up so quick that I barely have time to blink. Then, he slaps a handcuff on my wrist and the other on his own.

"I need rest and if you think I can trust you not to run away from me while I'm out of it, you're the crazy one. Now, get your sweet ass over in the bed so we can both get some sleep."

"You change so quickly, it makes my head spin."

"Got to keep you on your toes, Baby Girl."

Once we're settled on the bed, we both are quiet. I didn't think I could ever sleep, but one minute I'm closing my eyes, Chains body curling into me, spooning me from behind and the next I'm falling asleep, thinking I really like having his body so close to me.

I'm in deep trouble.

19

KAYDEN

I come awake slowly, my senses drugged from sleep. I kept waking up all night, probably because I was handcuffed to another person. It was either that or the fact that Chains was pressed up against me all night.

I've never slept with someone before. That, in and of itself, was completely new. But, sleeping with Chains was something else entirely. He seemed to fit against me like a glove. The heat of his body seemed to seep into my bones, wrapped around me and somehow made me feel safe. His arm stayed draped around me and his hand rested against my stomach.

All night.

Okay, that's a lie.

Somewhere in the middle of the night, his hand began drifting and rested against my breast. Chains didn't do anything overtly sexual, but it felt natural and I loved it. Somehow, him sleeping like that despite all the chaos made me feel cared for.

I'm probably insane.

This morning I have a choice. Chains is still out, he's got this soft snore that shouldn't be sexy, but it is. His breathing is even and when I rollover on my back, he does the same. He even manages to do it while still keeping that one hand on my stomach. It feels as if our bodies are in tune to one another.

And again, I've probably stepped on the crazy train.

Still, I'm fighting the urge to just give in. I want him and he's made no secret that he wants me. I have a feeling that I'm fighting a losing battle. It's going to happen. There's too much chemistry between us, too much physical attraction.

I'm just being stubborn. At first, it was because he had those women hanging all over him. Then, it was because he actually thought I went from him getting me off to sleeping with Thomas. Now, however, the complication is my father.

I don't know how to contain him. Hell, my mom has been with him for years and she hasn't managed to contain him. I think my father is one of a kind. He's a man that no one can tame, but he loves completely and no one will touch his family.

Not and live...

Dad would've had a hard time accepting any man I wanted. But, Chains kidnapping me, makes it impossible for Dad to ever accept him as...

What in the hell am I thinking? Chains isn't the type of man you could even call a boyfriend. That's not what this is; *that's not what this will ever be.* He kidnapped me, not because of some great love or relationship that he wants with me. He kidnapped me because he wants between my legs and he thought another man got there before him, after he'd already laid the groundwork. I need to remember that and not romanticize this shit. If anything, I am my father's daughter and I'm practical. At least, I always have been. I don't need to sentimentalize and daydream about a man who is only looking for a booty call.

No matter how fucking hot he is.

Still, I may be a booty call to him, but I care about Chains. He may not realize that, but I do. That means, I need to try and get out of here. The temptation is to stay here and at least have a taste of what I want, but doing that will get Chains killed.

Because, my father will kill him.

There might be a chance to save him if I could make my father listen to me, but that's easier said than done. My father will shoot first and then *maybe* ask questions as he's burying the body. That's who my daddy is, that's who he has always been. He doesn't try to hide that fact from us.

My parents have talked about the time my mother was kidnapped. I can see the emotion and the scars of that past on my father's face every time he thinks about it. Nothing and no one has ever been more important to my dad than my mom and his kids. I've always grown up secure in that knowledge.

That's how I know that Dad is not going to rest until he gets me back and he's not going to pull any punches to get revenge on Chains.

I can't stay here. I need to try and get ahead of this. I need to try and calm my father.

My mind made up, I'll start looking at my options. Chains and I slept in our clothes last night. I'll admit I was surprised he allowed that, and somewhere in the back of my mind a little disappointed.

That proves I'm insane, by the way.

I look at the cold metal on my wrist. My first task is to get that damn thing off. I'm going nowhere until I do. I watched Chains put the key in his pants pocket last night. I've never been good at pickpocketing, but then again, I've never really tried.

Desperation, it turns out, can be a great motivator. I turn my body and drape one leg over his, as if I'm hugging him up. I allow my free hand to hold him close. Chains mumbles in his sleep, but he doesn't move or wake. I give him a few minutes to settle and make sure he's still out. My eyes move around the mostly dark hotel room. There are a few soft strands of pale light coming through the closed curtains, which means it'll be daylight soon.

We must've slept forever; I thought for sure that I would have been awake earlier. I guess being kidnapped really tires you out. The thought makes me smile a little.

A girl has to keep her sense of humor.

When I'm sure that Chains is still sleeping, I let my hand slowly start moving towards his hip. I keep my gaze locked on his face the whole time, searching for movement or sound that he's playing me. You don't grow up with two older brothers and not get suspicious when a man is around. I let my finger slowly dip into the pocket opening. Chains mumbles under his breath and I freeze, thinking I've for sure been caught. I hold my body tense, preparing for the worst. I can hardly believe my luck when it appears he settles back into sleep.

Apparently kidnapping a biker princess takes a lot out of you, too.

Who knew?

I slide my finger deeper into the pocket, frowning when I don't feel a key. I push a little more, until my fingertips are pressed against the seam of his pocket.

"I think you need to move your fingers a little more to the right," Chains says, his voice sleepy and sinfully sexy. I ignore the chills of awareness it sends down my spine. Instead, I concentrate on the fact that I'm not going to get free today.

Then, I make the ultimate mistake. I look up at Chain's face.

He's sexy all the time, but with his hair mussed from sleeping, his blue eyes relaxed with slumber and sparkling with laughter, he's deadly. I instantly feel my body react to his smile, even though I shouldn't.

Shit...

20

CHAINS

"What you want isn't in my pocket," I grin.

"There's no key in your pocket," Kayden accuses, her voice soft, her eyes flashing with surprise.

I reach down and take her hand and move it to my cock—my hard, aching cock that is pushed up against the zipper of my jeans, demanding release. I cup my hand over hers, squeezing the hard edge of my shaft, pleasure curling through me like white-hot electricity.

"You don't really want a key, Kayden."

"I really do," she insists stubbornly, but when I take my hand away, hers stays pressed hard against my cock, her fingers pushing in as she squeezes me.

"Give me your mouth, Baby Girl."

"What if I don't want to?" she asks, her gaze locked on my lips, her eyes hungry.

"We both know you do."

"If I kiss you, it doesn't mean anything," she mumbles, her neck stretching as I dip down.

"It can mean everything," I tell her, my lips moving against hers.

"Shut up and kiss me, Chains," she growls.

That fucking growl wraps around my cock even tighter than her hand is right now. I kiss her, taking her mouth hard, swallowing her growl, and claiming her. The kiss is a series of tongues, teeth clashing, sucking, fighting for dominance. It's a war, not a kiss and I intend on winning. Kayden submits to me, melting in my arms, her fingers busy unbuttoning my pants.

"Don't start something you're not willing to finish, Kayden," I moan, breaking away from her mouth, just to kiss down her neck and let my teeth scrape against her tender skin.

"I'd be finishing it, if you'd quit talking," she argues, her head going back to encourage me to keep tasting her sweet skin.

Somehow the little minx has managed to get my cock free. Her hand wraps back around it, stroking me and squeezing me tight. It feels so fucking good, I could come just from that alone. She moves then to flip us, so that she's lying on top of me. I growl, moving our joined hands because they get trapped between us.

"Take off the handcuff, Chains."

"Stop talking and get to fucking," I mutter against her shoulder, biting down against the skin and marking it.

She pulls back and looks at me, surprise on her face. A startled laugh escapes from her as she looks at me.

"Damn, Chains, your sweet talk is on point," she jokes.

"I need you naked, and as much as I like the way you give me attitude, I have much better things in mind for that mouth of yours, Baby Girl."

"Undo my handcuff and I'll rock your world."

"How about you just make my world unsteady and I leave the handcuff on?" I smirk. I know what her game is and I'm willing to play along, but I'm not giving her everything. She's too fucking used to getting her way. That's where I went wrong the first time. Now, she needs to learn who is in charge.

"Are you kidding me right now?" she huffs.

"I'm trying to fuck you."

"Then nix this," she says, shaking our joined hands.

"Maybe after you earn it."

Her eyes dilate and I see the minute my words not only hit her, they spark her anger.

"You're completely insane."

"I am right now. My girl is giving me a case of blue balls."

"You're lucky I'm not kneeing you in the balls," she barks. "I can't believe you, right now. That's it. I'm done. D.O.N.E."

"Does that mean we're not going to fuck?"

"We are *never* going to fuck," she says shaking her head, starting to slide off my body. "In fact, if I ever see your dick come near me, I'll grab a knife and cut it off!"

I wrap my arm around her, not allowing her to move.

"We most definitely are going to fuck, Kayden. And, for the record, by the time I'm done with you, you'll be begging for my cock."

"You're dreaming."

"I'm just telling the truth."

"If you think that's the truth, then you're delusional as well as certifiable."

"You're going to be begging for my cock soon, Kayden."

"I will not," she insists stubbornly.

"I always did like a challenge," I tell her and then I lean up and take her mouth again in a quick, hard kiss.

I don't stop until her body softens and she finally gives in, kissing me back. I end it just as it starts getting good. When she opens those deep chocolate brown eyes of hers, I'm grinning in victory.

She mutters under her breath and I let her go this time.

I'm already planning my attack for tonight, though. In the back of my mind I'm wondering why I find this back and forth with her more exciting than anything I've ever had with another woman—including sex.

Kayden West is a fucking dangerous woman, but it's too late to worry about that now.

I'm in too deep...

21

KAYDEN

"What is this place?" I ask, looking around at what looks like a scene from a B-movie.

"This is where you and I are going to come to an understanding."

I slide out of the vehicle, standing slowly. My legs are so sore from hours of riding without stopping, that my first step is like an 80-year-old woman recovering from a hip replacement.

I look at the small, wood siding cabin. It's an A frame set back in the woods and the kind that are in those campy horror movies. Movies where a bunch of camp counselors are fucking and get beheaded...

We are still somewhere in the state of Virginia, but I have no idea where. We stopped for what supplies a while back and I didn't ask a lot of questions—I was just glad he didn't make me wear handcuffs in the store.

When we got back in the car, there were so many turns and backroads with twists that I couldn't keep up. I figure that's the way Chains wanted it, and eventually I just gave up. I do know the driveway that we turned off of was a dirt road that seemed to go on for-freaking-ever. It's very secluded. If I wasn't worried about my father showing up, killing Chains and going to jail, I might even like it.

Chains hasn't said much since we left the hotel. He drove straight through the night again and I didn't complain. We don't seem to be driving in any way that makes since to me, but I figure he has some weird plan and as long as there's not a trail my father can find, I'm okay with it. At least that gives me a little time to figure out how to fix this situation. So far, I've come up with nothing that might help, other than I need to get away from Chains and stop my father's head hunting.

On the trip here, every now and then Chains would reach over and touch my face or my hand. When I looked at him, he would be smiling. I have no idea how to read him, or what is going through his mind. He's unlike any man I've ever known and while I know I'm a virgin, I grew up around a lot of bikers and men of that lifestyle. You would think I'd be able to at least get a handle on who Chains is.

"This place looks like the backdrop for a horror film," I share. "If you turn out to be a serial killer, Chains, I've got to warn you of something."

"What's that?"

"If you kill me, I will come back and haunt your ass for the rest of your life."

"Oh, Kayden, my little drama queen. I don't have that on my to do list. Unless, you can die from an overload of orgasms, because I plan on giving you a lot of those," he laughs.

He comes around to my side of the car and picks me up in his arms. I squeal, because the move was so unexpected. I hold onto him in surprise, but being honest with myself, I melt into his body. I love being in his arms.

I love being with him...

"Isn't carrying me over the threshold kind of a big commitment for our relationship?" I ask as he takes us into the cabin.

"Does this mean you're finally accepting that we have a relationship?" he replies with a smirk.

"I think kidnapping is a pretty huge relationship really," I respond sarcastically.

"I warned you early on that I wasn't the kind of man you toyed with. If it takes getting you alone, away from the boy toys that you are used to, then so be it. I'll do what I have to do to get in there with you."

He puts me down on the floor, but he keeps my body close to him as his finger goes underneath my chin. I have to tilt my head under the pressure, forced to look up at him. He stares at me for long minutes, as if he's searching for something. I don't take my eyes off of him either, maybe I'm searching for something too.

"Are you saying, you kidnapped me, drove me through God knows how many counties in the state of Virginia, made sure my father would find a way to kill your ass, and you did all of this because you didn't want me screwing another man?" I ask him, not sure how to make sense out of this entire situation.

"Is that so hard to believe? I told you I didn't share. What did you think was going to happen when I saw you with that kid?"

"That kid is older than I am, Chains."

"He's still a kid, and you, Kayden West, are a complete handful. You need a man, Baby, not some wet behind the ears boy."

"And you've decided you're that man?"

"You decided that the minute you let me between those legs."

"Maybe I did, let's say for the sake of an argument, that I decided you were the man I wanted in my bed – – at least for a little while," I admit, although qualifying my answer. "I would say that all bets were off the minute I found you standing with two women draped all over you. You said that you didn't share, Chains. Remember? Well, neither do I."

"So you fucked that kid, out of jealousy, because you thought you needed to get revenge. That's fucked up, Kayden, but I guess I can understand it. I'm not happy about it. I'm pretty fucking pissed in general, and I can't promise I won't snap that kid's neck if I ever see him again. But you and me, we'll work this out here, just the two of us. No one else will be in play here. It will just be you and me."

He pulls his shirt off, taking a step back from me, his gaze locked onto mine, as if daring me to argue.

"You're really unbelievable, do you know that?"

"That's nice of you to notice," he mocks, throwing his shirt on the floor.

"Have you ever heard of talking to a woman?"

"What is between us will be better said without words, if you catch my drift."

"That's so stupid," I laugh, finally turning away from him. I walk to a chair that has been covered up by a sheet. I pull the dusty fabric off, wrinkling my nose as I get the urge to sneeze. Then, I throw it on the floor and sit down. My gaze automatically lifting to Chains again. His hands are at his belt, and I shake my head no.

"If you are going to deny that you want me, that you don't want *us*, Kayden, you can save your breath."

"If you think it is so easy for me to go from what we did together and then, give myself to another man, why even bother with me? Why not go back to your club whores? Better yet, why even care? I mean, what happened to the old saying what's good for the goose, is good for the gander?"

"I have no idea where farm animals come into this shit. For the record, I'm not into that level of kink. But, if you're asking me why you getting into bed with that kid wasn't a deal breaker, I have no fucking idea. I just know, what I feel for you is something I haven't had before and I'm not willing to let it go, at least not yet. As for those women at the club, they were nothing."

My heart is pounding in my chest. I do my best not to let it show. I don't want him to know that he's getting to me, but his words have me shaking. He just admitted that he has feelings for me.

Okay, I'm young and inexperienced in this crap, but I don't think a man like Chains admits to having feelings for someone easily. I don't know what it means, but I know how it makes me feel… *how he makes me feel.*

"It didn't look like nothing from where I was sitting."

"That's because you left too soon to see what happened."

"If I had stayed, what would I have seen?" I ask him, feeling like this conversation right now is extremely important. I curl my hand and let my fingernails dig into my palm as I try to understand how Chains' mind works.

"Me pushing them away to get to you. I only wanted to stop you from leaving with him."

His gaze is trained on me. The whole time he is talking he's deadly serious and doubts begin to leave me. I don't know why I believe him, but I truly don't think Chains cheated on me. I don't think he had anything to do with those Twinkies. Once I acknowledge that, it feels like a giant weight has been lifted off my shoulders.

But, I'm not about to let him off the hook that easily.

"Then, if that's really what would've happened—"

"That is one hundred percent what happened, Kayden."

"Then, maybe you should've stopped them from hanging all over you in the first place and this wouldn't have been a problem."

"Are you feeling territorial over me, Baby Girl?"

"Stop being so full of yourself. I'm pointing out that if you had stopped that, we wouldn't have a problem. It sure wouldn't have gotten to the point you *kidnapped* me. If anyone is being territorial here, it's you, Chains."

"I fully admit I'm territorial over you, Kayden. You're mine. I told you that when you came all over my fingers. And, just to remind you, you didn't know anything about those women when you were there to pick your toy up," he counters. "So, we would still have had problems."

"And this is why you should have come into my apartment and talked to me. Not act like a fucking caveman."

"I tried that. If you remember, you wouldn't listen and you didn't want me there. I took the only option I had."

"Maybe you should've led with I didn't do anything with those women. Maybe that would've helped, instead of yelling about Thomas."

I am feeling extremely guilty, because, he's right. I didn't exactly give him a chance to explain. My mother always says that I inherited my father's temper. I always deny it, but I know that she's right. I usually react and then regret it later.

Much like now...Only this time my actions might be enough to get Chains killed.

"And maybe, you should be the one to listen when your man talks."

I roll my eyes. "You're so full of yourself. I listen when there's something worth listening to. And you don't really explain or talk as much as you tell me how it's going to be and what is going to happen. In case you haven't noticed yet, I'm a grown ass woman. I don't need a man to tell me how things are going to be. I need a man who is secure enough to talk things over with me and let us decide *together*."

"Is that what your toy lets you do? I think you need a man to reel you in. Because, God knows, you've been running free for way too long."

"You did *not* just say that to me."

"I'll say it again if you have a hard time understanding, Baby Girl."

"You have no idea what you're talking about," I laugh.

"I know that you have your daddy wrapped around your finger and he lets you run way too fucking free."

"Now you're just insane. My father nearly smothers me to death. My brothers, on the other hand, are wild and free. I'm the one barely allowed to go inside his precious club. Hell, I barely go to the movies unless someone is with me."

"Have you looked at yourself Kayden? Baby Girl, you're walking sex on a stick. I don't have kids, and I don't figure they're in the cards for me."

"Especially now," I mutter, thinking my father will take great pleasure it cutting off every appendage Chains has.

"But," he continues, giving me an annoyed look. "If I had a girl who looked like you, there's no fucking way in hell that I would let her roam free as much as your father lets you."

"Say what?" I ask wondering if I should kiss him or shoot him.

"I didn't stutter. If I had a daughter, that looked one half as hot as you, I would lock her up. I'd definitely keep her out of reach of old bastard's like me."

"You realize you don't make a bit of sense, right?"

"You're just mad because you know I'm right," he says with an easy smile that warms me from the inside out.

"You think you know everything don't you, Chains?"

"About you? I think I'm barely scratching the surface. But, everything I've learned makes me want to know more," he says, his voice gruff. His reply makes my heart stutter in my chest.

Chains is not a man to give flowery compliments. He's plain spoken and rude to the point of being obnoxious. In a lot of ways, he reminds me of my father and maybe that's why I like him so much. Because, I know that when he gives a compliment he truly means it. What he just said feels huge.

"I bet I can tell you something about me that you don't know."

"Surprise me, Baby."

"Dom and Thomas aren't my boy toys or whatever you call it."

"No offense, Baby Girl, but I don't want to hear about the men who came before me. I plan on fucking them out of your head."

"That won't be hard to do," I laugh.

"I like that you have confidence in me, I don't plan on disappointing you."

He looks so happy, so self-satisfied with himself, that I have to laugh. He is as cocky as hell, but damn it, I like that too.

"You are so damn full of yourself."

"I can't wait until you're full of me," he says with a smirk.

"Aren't you the least interested in finding out what you don't know about me, Chains?"

"I figure I could spend years and never find out everything."

"Damn, you really can be smooth when you try." He doesn't respond to that, he just grins. "You probably don't have years with me, however. I figure my father is close on our trail even now."

"You might be right, but this place is off the grid enough that I'm willing to take my chances."

He's underestimating my father, but I let it go. I'm going to have tonight with him. After that... I need to find out a way to save Chains' life.

"What if I told you that those boy toys are my brothers?"

I see the minute my words hit him. I see the surprise on his face and I smile in victory.

"Maybe you should have told me that before I kidnapped you," he barks.

I throw my head back and straight out laugh, because it's not like he was letting me say much of anything and I was so mad over the Twinkies I wouldn't have told him the truth anyway. If Chains is hard headed then someone should warn him that I'm worse.

I wasn't watching so I'm not prepared for the way he charges over and picks me up, throwing me over his shoulder.

"What are you doing now?" I ask, still laughing.

"I'm going to fuck you until you can't use that sweet mouth of yours to sass me."

"That might take a while," I warn him.

He grunts in reply, making me laugh some more.

Damn it, I really like this biker.

I like him way too much.

22

CHAINS

There's only one bedroom in this small cabin. There's a large cloth tarp over the bed. It's dusty and needs a good cleaning. I would have preferred to have it clean before I take Kayden, but I can't wait and she doesn't seem to be pushing me away—or giving me hell with that smart mouth of hers—so I'm not about to wait. My girl seems to change depending on which way the wind blows. That thought makes me smile. She's the first woman I can ever remember who keeps me on my toes, always does something to surprise me, and doesn't fucking bore me.

I can't imagine Kayden ever boring me.

I help her to stand when we get in front of the bed. She looks around, frowning.

"I don't suppose I could talk you into cleaning—"

I don't let her finish. I take her mouth in mine, showing her without words how much I fucking want her. When we break apart I'm groaning and she's licking her lips making it worse. I've got to have her and soon. I can't hold back much longer.

"You really know how to kiss," she murmurs. I barely catch

her words, instead I'm focused on the way the tip of her tongue slips out to run against her lip.

I reach behind her to pull the tarp away from the bed. There's a bare mattress and I'm just thankful it appears clean.

"Undress, Kayden."

"Uh... maybe we should think about this," she hedges, but I shake my head no. The time for thinking is over.

"Undress."

"Just like that?" she squeaks, almost sounding afraid.

"You have a problem with that?"

"It seems a little unfair. I mean *you're* completely dressed."

"And?" I ask, enjoying the annoyance that flashes in her eyes.

"How about a little tit for tat?" she mumbles avoiding my eyes.

"Trust me, Baby Girl, I definitely plan on getting your tits... I wouldn't exactly call them little, though. Damn, a man could smother in those beauties and die a happy man."

"God, you're such a pig," she says shaking her head, but she's laughing.

"Oink, oink," I respond, grinning. "Okay fine, let's do it your way," I tell her and I start by kicking off my boots. "Your turn."

Her eyes narrow as she looks at me. I relax my stance, making the unspoken dare clear to her. For a minute, I think she will back down. Then, she surprises me by kicking off the sandals on her feet. "Fine," she huffs.

She's beautiful. Defiance wrapped up in a package so damn fuckable my dick aches. I can't believe I'm finally going to have her. The only problem now is if I'll be able to let her go afterwards. Suddenly, I'm pretty sure that answer is no... as in *no-fucking-way*.

I use my feet to shuffle out of my socks, and wait to see her next move—since she's not wearing socks. She frowns at me, but takes off a bracelet she's wearing and places it on the sheet that's covering the dresser.

"I don't think that can be called clothes, Kayden."

She shrugs like she doesn't give a damn and gives me a pointed look.

I take off my cut and drape it across the footboard. She purses her lips like that annoyed her.

"You have more clothes than me," she says finally.

"So?"

"That means I'll be naked way before you. That's not good enough."

"You realize how fucking stupid that is right? Before this is done, Kayden, both of us are going to be as naked as the day we were born."

"I'm going to pick one article of clothing I keep on until... well during the festivities."

My head drops. My smile trembles with the urge to laugh, but I'm trying to hold it in. I'm starting to get the message here that she's sending without realizing it. Kayden is a virgin. For all her sass and attitude, I can see how unsure she is of herself and the flashes of panic. I let that information filter in my brain. I allow the knowledge to sift through me. I should call an end to this. Deliver her back to her family, walk away and keep walking. She's too young, too special for a man who has spent his life on the back of a bike avoiding responsibility like it was the plague. I've always lived for freedom. That's who I am. If the clubs that I've visited all have creeds, words they live by, then so do I—mine is just vastly different.

No ties, no obligations, no regrets.

Kayden... she's definitely wrapped around me, tying herself to me with invisible ropes that I have no hope of breaking. I know that going through with this, taking her body, definitely makes me obligated, because Kayden deserves a man who takes her innocence with care, and someone who will continue to care about her, even once her virginity is gone. If I don't have my taste of her, if I don't try and tie her to me, claim her and make her mine, then instinctively, I know I will regret it for the rest of my life.

Suddenly I've become a man who once didn't believe in responsibility, to a man who wants nothing more than to care for and cherish this woman for the rest of my life.

Which most likely won't be long, once her father catches up to me.

Even that sad fact hasn't been enough to make me walk away from her and it still isn't.

"Chains?" Kayden prompts me, her voice questioning, but also betraying a little of her nerves.

"You pick one article of clothing to stay on, Kayden," I tell her, letting her think I'm giving in.

"Just like that?" she asks, her face clearing, her lips moving into a smile and her body instantly relaxing.

"Just like that," I agree.

"Then," she whispers, her smile deepening and a look that can only be described as victory coming across her face. "I choose my underwear."

"Fair enough," I tell her.

She frowns. "That's my bra *and* my panties," she warns me.

"I know what underwear is, Kayden."

"Then, I... I'm not sure how this is going to work," she mumbles, still frowning.

"That's not for you to worry about. Trust me, Baby, I'll make this work," I tell her and then just because I can, I pull off my shirt and throw it on the floor. Kayden pulls hers off next and follows suit when I take my pants off as well.

"You're covered in ink," she murmurs, her eyes glued to my chest and arms.

"You like it?"

She doesn't reply, her gaze slowly travels downward. Her body jerks and I know the exact moment she sees my cock, heavy with need, bobbing out toward her, wanting her. I have a large cock, I never thought much of it either way. The ladies seem to like it and I just thanked the Man above that it wasn't some three-inch pencil dick they'd laugh and run from. Then again, I've never dealt with a virgin before. I allowed her to keep herself covered up because I didn't want to see any fear on her face, but I see it now as she takes in my engorged cock, the head slickened and wet, full of need and hunger.

"I... Chains, I don't think this is going to work," she whispers, taking a step away from me.

I close up that distance quickly, wrapping my hand against the side of her neck.

"It's not only going to work, Kayden, I promise you by the time it's over you'll be begging for more."

She stares at me for a minute and I watch as she beats down her fear.

"I'm not really a begging type of girl. Maybe I'll make *you* beg," she says.

"That's my girl. Give me that fire, Kayden. I want it and I can promise you, Baby Girl, if you burn me with it, I'll enjoy begging for more," I growl before claiming her mouth. She melts in my arms as my tongue takes over her mouth.

Each time I kiss her, it seems to get better. Each time I have a taste of her, I'm left wondering how I ever survived without her...

23

KAYDEN

I know I've made a fool of myself. Instead of making me feel self-conscious, somehow Chains managed to put me at ease —at least until I got a look at his cock.

His fully aroused cock.

Sweet Baby Jesus, that thing is probably labeled as a deadly weapon in at least twenty states, maybe more. It's wide and thick and so long it can't even stand up at attention. It bobs out, too big to even support its own weight. I'm torn between wanting to see how it feels inside of me—how *Chains* feels inside of me—and wanting to run in the opposite direction. I've never had sex before, so I can only guess, but I'm pretty sure virgins aren't able to handle that much dick.

I forget about the size of his dick while he's kissing me, but once we break away from each other it's the first thing I remember.

"How... I mean, do you know... Well, like in inches or whatever..." I stutter, trailing off because I'm not sure how to put into words what I want to know.

"Baby Girl," Chains says in a warning voice—which is just annoying. I look back up at him.

"It's a legitimate question considering you want to put that *thing* in me."

"You've yet to ask me a question, Kayden."

"Okay fine!" I huff out. "How big is it?" I'm looking down at my feet, which means my gaze goes straight to his dick and I step back away from him quickly.

"What?" he practically barks.

"You heard me. I've got to tell you, Chains, I don't think that thing's going to fit in me."

"It'll fit," he laughs, closing in on me and causing me to step back again.

"I'm not so sure. Do you have numbers?"

"Numbers?" he asks, looking at me confused. I take the opportunity to take a couple more steps away.

"Of the women you've been with before, so I can ask their opinions."

Chains doesn't say anything. He just stands there looking at me, blinking.

"Well?" I prompt him when he doesn't reply.

"I wouldn't give you numbers of women that came before you, even if I knew them," he grumbles.

"I see..."

"What exactly do you see?"

"You're afraid to let me talk to them, because they'll prove what I already know."

"What's that, for Christ's sake?"

"That you did irreparable harm to them and they're in nursing homes drooling, unable to talk and confined to a wheelchair, unable to walk because they were drilled by the King Kong lizard you're carrying between your legs."

"Lizard?" he barks, like he can't believe what I just said. I should have probably warned him that when I'm nervous I just say the first thing that pops into my mind, but I didn't and I'm pretty sure the cat is out of the bag now.

"I'm too young to be put in a home. I just don't think—"

I stop talking, mostly because I'm too busy squealing as Chains grabs me, lifts me up, and then tosses me on the bed like I'm nothing more than a sack of potatoes.

"Kayden, Baby, shut those beautiful lips of yours. I'm about to show you so much pleasure you'll be begging for more," he tells me and he's smiling down at me in such a way that I kind of believe him.

Kind of...

"You promise you'll go slow?"

"Slower than you'll want me to," he promises.

"And if it hurts you'll stop."

"I promise that if it hurts, it won't last long and the pleasure will be worth it," he qualifies.

I frown, pulling my gaze away from him and looking up at the ceiling instead.

"Why couldn't I be attracted to a man with a teeny weenie?" I ask the powers that be.

They, of course, don't answer.

Sigh.

24

KAYDEN

"Christ you're cute," he growls, getting on the bed, his knees pressed into the mattress, sitting between my legs.

"I'm nervous," I admit instead, suddenly feeling very out of my element.

"There's no need to be nervous with me, Kayden. You're safe with me."

"It's not you, Chains. I'd be nervous if I was with any man right now."

That apparently was the wrong thing to say.

His hand slides against my neck and he pulls me until our noses are almost touching.

"I'm not just any man, Kayden. I'm *your* man. I'm the one you chose to give your body to. I know how special that is," he says.

His eyes are so intense, they seem to burn into me and I know that no matter how old I am, or what happens in my life, that I won't regret this moment.

"I really should have been all cool and just undressed for you and said let's get it over with. I'm not weak because I'm a little afraid, you know."

"Baby Girl, a man would have to be a complete idiot to think you could ever be weak."

I can tell he means that and the emotion I feel at what sounds like *pride* in his voice, is hard to explain. It gives me courage like nothing else could.

I pull back, then reach between us and unlatch my bra—letting it fall to the floor. I fight the urge to hide my breasts with my hand. *This is it.* This is the moment that I've been waiting for and even if I didn't know it at the time, I was waiting for Chains.

"You're so fucking beautiful, Baby," he murmurs, and I feel my skin heat at the compliment—and at the way he's staring at my breasts. My nipples harden, tightening even more the longer he stares at them. I look away, feeling so many different emotions that I don't know how to deal with it. That could have been a mistake, because I'm not prepared when Chains begins kissing down my neck.

"I… That feels good," I whisper, tilting my head to give him better access. His lips feel soft, his breath heated and when his tongue slips out and touches my skin, I bite my lip to keep from moaning—I still do, but not as loud as I would have.

"You taste so fucking good, Kayden," Chains whispers against my skin, his voice hoarse, rumbly and it makes me wet and my center spasm in reaction. Chains should definitely come with a warning label.

Caution. Could be addicting.

I feel like I should be doing something, but my mind is too full of thoughts that I can't grasp, all I can do is feel. Instead, my fingers bite into Chains back, my body shifting restlessly, wanting more but unable to put it into words. It doesn't matter because he seems to know. His lips move down, leaving a heated trail in their wake. I feel his hand hold one of my breasts and then his tongue dances along the hardened nipple. I gasp in shock, my body going stiff and then he sucks the nipple into his mouth and I moan out as pleasure so intense hits me that my eyes close. I hold onto him, because I have no choice. Suddenly, Chains has become the center of my universe.

I'm so lost in the magic that his lips are creating that I lose track of the way his hand is moving. That is until it slips beneath my panties and spreads the lips of my pussy. I know I'm extremely wet, realize that even my panties are wet and I can feel my juices gathering on his fingers instantly with just the barest touch. I should be embarrassed, but I'm not. Instead, my legs seem to spread without my knowing and I open myself up even more to him.

"That's my good girl," he whispers against my breast. "So eager to please me."

I don't argue with him, I do want to please him. I want to do anything I can that will ensure that whatever else happens, Chains doesn't stop touching me. I don't want him to stop delivering the pleasure that he is right now.

His finger slides against my clit and my body literally jolts as this hunger, so intense it tears through me, takes over.

"More, Chains. Please," I whimper, not even recognizing my own voice.

"I got you, Kayden, I got you," he croons. Then, a second finger joins the first and I close my eyes, imaging his fingers based on the way I feel them. They're moving in a circular movement, caressing and enticing. My hips begin to move as I ride his hand. I'm so wet now that I can literally hear his fingers move against my pussy and even that doesn't embarrass me. It makes me want more.

"Touch me, Kayden. Stroke me and see how hard you make your man," he says and God, it sounds like he's practically begging. A man like Chains, he doesn't have to beg for anything and the fact that he's giving me this, it's more than a gift. It feels priceless and all nerves are gone as I reach down and take his cock in my hand and begin clumsily pumping it. I'm emboldened when Chains' hoarse growl of approval rings out and I stroke him faster.

"Chains," I whimper, asking for something, anything because I feel like I'm on the edge and I just need him to fix it. I need him to push me over, give me what I know in my heart that only he can.

"My girl ready for more?" he purrs against my breast and when I don't answer he captures it between his teeth and bites. Pain and pleasure mingle, making me cry out, my body convulsing with desire.

"Chains," I call, a wave of hunger shoots through me.

I hear the tearing of fabric, I'm too far gone to know what it is or even means. My hand is holding onto Chains' cock, so tight that if I had the presence of mind to think, I'd worry I was hurting him. Then, his hand caps over mine. I still don't understand. I just cry out, because he's no longer playing with my clit. He applies pressure and then we're stroking his cock together. I open my mouth to speak, but I can only breathe out, as I feel his precum run against my fingers. I open my eyes slowly and find myself staring into his deep, Prussian blue eyes that are dilated and filled with yearning.

Yearning for me... *for us.*

25

CHAINS

I position my cock at her entrance, both our hands still holding me. This startled look comes across Kayden's face.

"My panties," she murmurs, a shocked giggle bursting out.

"You're still wearing them, Baby Girl. They just aren't in my way now."

I smile, kissing her lips briefly once, then twice and sucking her bottom lip into my mouth, teasing it with my tongue and hoping to distract her from what comes next.

I'm going so damn slow here that my balls are in pain. I need to fuck her and I need to come, but I don't want to rush this. I want to do everything in my power to make sure she's ready. I know that she's going to feel pain, but I want to make sure that she also feels pleasure. Kissing her like this, drinking from her lips feels good, nice and when her tongue comes out to play and touch against mine, I feel like I've reached my goal. She's enjoying this and not worrying about anything else.

I let the head of my cock rub against her clit, then I push against it, because that feels good too. She stares up at me and I get lost in her eyes, loving the way she's looking as if I was the most precious thing in life to her. Suddenly, I realize, that's exactly what I want to be.

Emotions hit me that I've never felt before.

Love.

I've never believed in it before, but right now that's exactly what I'm feeling. I start to tell her that right then. The words are there, but for some reason, I push them back, concentrating instead on pushing the head of my cock inside her.

"Oh," she puffs out with a small exhale of air. Shock and wonder are equally laced in her voice. "Wow."

"Feels good, don't it, Baby?" I all but moan, letting go of her lips. She's looking at me again with awe and I do my best to control my heartbeat which is pounding in my chest.

"I feel… full…" she responds, as I slip just a little deeper.

"You are full, Kayden, you're full of me," I tease her, shocked that in this moment, where I know I'm in love with a woman and that I'm having the best sex I'll ever have in my life, that one of the overriding emotions is happiness.

Kayden gives me that.

She is pure joy.

"It feels good, Chains. *You* feel good," she says, as I slip inside of her tight little pussy just a little more. I stop when she frowns, afraid that I'm causing her pain. I'm pushing against her virginity. One thrust and she's finally mine, but I need to make sure she's okay before I go forward.

"You're too big," she whispers. "Will it work like this?" I'm confused at first, but then I feel her hook her leg over mine, the heel of her foot pressing against the back of my leg, as she moves her hips to try and ride me. "Help me," she mumbles, sounding upset with me.

It's then I realize that she thinks this is it. She thinks this is as far as I can get inside of her. I've been going too slow, trying to spare her any pain that I can, when maybe the opposite was needed.

"This will only hurt for a minute," I promise her.

Before she can ask me anything else, I thrust all the way inside of her, burying myself in her sweet cunt all the way to the hilt. The muscles of her pussy flex all around my shaft, which is hard as steel.

She cries out and I feel like a bastard, but I love every second of it. Once I'm pushing against her womb, possessing her and knowing that I'm the only man to feel how fucking good this is, I don't move. It's pure torture, not fucking her hard, and bathing her in cum, but I don't. I know she's hurting. I feel it in the way her body is stiff against mine, in her labored breathing, and in the way her fingernails are biting into my skin.

"Shhh..." I murmur, kissing her temple, perspiration dotting her skin. "It's okay now, Kayden. I promise it will only get better from here on out."

I keep my voice soft, trying to soothe her, feeling out of my depth, because as much as this is new for her, it's also new to me. I've never cared like this, never belonged to another human being in the way that I belong to Kayden.

"Chains," she says, her voice sounding strained. I hold my weight on one arm, and even that small movement shifts my dick inside of her and I groan at how fucking good just that small movement feels.

"It's okay, Baby Girl. It'll all feel good again in a minute," I tell her, hoping to hell that I'm right. I don't think I can hold back very much longer.

"I think you're too big," she whispers, her voice strained.

Carefully, I begin playing with her breasts again, massaging them, teasing the nipple. I use my tongue to tease the hard peaks, as I let my hand move between us and search out her clit.

I massage it, while letting my tongue lave her nipple, offering silent praise when her body softens underneath me and begins to move.

"I like that," she whispers.

"Then, I'll give you more," I tell her. "I'll always give you anything to keep you happy, Kayden."

"Then, maybe you should move," she keens, frustrated.

"How does this feel?" I ask, tentatively as I begin to move, still playing with her clit. A wave of slick juices running against my fingers is an answer long before her whispered answer.

"So good. I need more, Chains."

"That's my girl," I praise, beginning to move with more purpose, fucking her body in a way that I know both of us will get what we want sooner.

"Wrong," she groans, her body beginning to move with mine as I show her the rhythm to ride out her climax that I can feel begin in her body.

"What?" I ask, watching as pleasure moves over her face.

"I'm not your girl," she says on a gasp, her entire body shuddering. I can see and feel the exact moment the orgasm takes her over and I pick up my speed, needing to fuck her hard, wanting to bathe her womb in my cum, needing to claim her in the most elemental way possible.

"Kayden—"

"I'm your woman, now," she cries, her head going back as she yells the words and I sure as fuck don't plan on correcting her. Instead, I fuck her until we both come and I don't stop until I've emptied myself completely in her and hoping against hope that I've planted my child inside of her.

26

CHAINS

"You're quiet," Kayden purrs in my ear.

I'm lying on my back, she's on her side, her body pressed tight against me, one leg stretched over me, her head on my arm and her fingers dancing across the skin on my neck.

"I'm sorry, Baby Girl."

"What are you thinking?" she asks and if nothing else, I owe her the truth.

"I was thinking that tonight was probably the single most beautiful thing I could ever imagine," I respond, turning to look at her.

"Chains..." she replies her dark eyes deepening with emotion to the point that they seem to sparkle.

"I knew you were going to be trouble, Kayden, but I had no idea," I tell her and because I'm unable to stop myself, I lean in and touch our lips together briefly before pulling away and moving my thumb against her bottom lip.

"I need to talk to you about that."

"No, you don't."

"I do, Chains. You have to know that my father is busy trying to find me, even now."

"He is and I figure eventually he will, but he doesn't get to enter into this, Kayden."

"This? Chains, he's *all* in this."

"Not these moments, Baby Girl. Not now. While we're together like this the only thing in this whole fucking world that exists is me and you. No one else, nothing else."

"I wish that were true," she says sadly.

"It is. I'm not sharing you with anyone or anything else, Kayden. You're inexperienced, but you have to know what happened between us just now isn't something that just happens. It was fucking—"

"Phenomenal," she says with a sweet smile that lights up her whole face, making her glow with happiness and pleasure.

I feel like I'm fucking ten feet tall, because I'm the man that gave that to her. Her hand comes up to mine, her fingers moving between mine and pulling my thumb away from her face. I pull so our joined hands come to my mouth and kiss her hand gently.

"It was special, so fucking special I think only a handful of people ever get to experience it."

"Wow, Chains, what has happened to you? You're suddenly sounding sweet," she murmurs.

"I'm not letting you go, Kayden," I vow.

"Chains, we can't..."

"I'm not letting you go, Kayden," I tell her again, and just so she can't doubt me, I move her so she's forced to slide over my body, lying on me. Her hair spills around her face, her eyes darken with hunger and she grinds against my already hardening dick. I don't know how the fucker is ready to go after the workout he just got, but I don't give a damn either. I have a feeling I will never get enough of Kayden—*ever*.

"I'm going to have to go home, Chains. You know that."

"Not for a while and when you do, I'll go with you."

"No," she says, panic on her face. "You can't do that. He'll kill you. You don't know my father, he reacts first and thinks years down the road—at least when it comes to his family. You can't go back, at least not until I manage to tame his temper."

"You'll have to tame it quick if that's your plan, Baby Girl, because I'm not leaving you."

"Chains, what are you saying?"

"I'm saying that what we just shared in this room together is something that I'm never—*never* going to give up. I claimed you, I put my mark on you, but you did the same to me."

"Chains, stop for a moment and just think—"

"I'm keeping you."

"Keeping me?" she asks, her eyes going round.

"I'm not letting you go, Kayden, ever."

"Chains, you're being crazy. You can't just keep a person. I have a life in Kentucky and you're always on the road—"

"If you're in Kentucky, then I will be too."

"I... I don't know what to say to this," she whispers, and I can see unshed tears gathering in her eyes. One tear starts to leak from the corner and I wipe it away with my thumb before it can fall and then bring it to my mouth to taste it.

"There's nothing to say, Kayden. If you think I'm going to let you go and risk another man claiming what you gave to me, you're insane. I'm not giving you away. I'm not letting another man put a hand on what is mine."

"Maybe we should just take this one day at a time," she says, running her teeth along the bottom of her lip.

"Take it however you need to take it, just realize that what I'm telling you is the truth."

"The problem with that is we don't have a lot of time," she says. "Do you swear there's no way my father can find us?"

"I wouldn't know how. No one knows about this place but an old buddy of mine and he's currently stationed in South Korea. Even if your father did manage to trace our steps, finding this cabin is next to impossible. There's no real road to it and none you will find on any GPS regardless."

"Then, let's take it day by day and make sure this is what you want... that I'm what you want," she says.

I can't stop myself so I claim her mouth, kissing her with all of the emotion I'm feeling, rubbing my cock against her, letting her feel exactly how much I want her.

"I'm already completely sure you're what I want, Kayden, but if it will take you a few days to realize it, I can wait."

"That's so nice of you," she says sarcastically.

"Quit talking and guide me inside that sweet pussy of yours, woman."

"I'm sore," she warns me, but her hand is already eagerly stroking my cock as she shifts to guide me inside of her.

"We'll go slow, Baby, and I promise to kiss it better afterwards," I tell her, moaning the last part as she squeezes my cock in a downward stroke.

"Quit talking, Chains," she mutters, reaching up to press our lips together at the exact moment she aligns our bodies perfectly and begins to slide down on my cock.

I close my eyes thinking only one thing.

Kayden West is heaven on earth...

27

DRAGON

"Dragon, you're going to have to try and come to bed and sleep a little bit."

"I can't sleep, Mama."

"If you don't start taking care of yourself, you're going to get sick. That's not going to help Kayden."

"Sleeping sure as fuck isn't going to help her, Nicole," I growl, frustrated as hell. I sit down on the bed, giving my woman my back, staring out into the darkness. I feel the bed shift behind me, but I don't turn and give her my attention. I'm too damn keyed up to be the man she needs. I should be the one trying to reassure her—not the other way around. Then I feel her body press against my back, her arms go around me and she squeezes me in a hug. My head drops down and I bring my hand up to cap over hers.

"I love you, Dragon."

"I'm sorry, Mama."

"What are you sorry for?"

"It's been a week and I've yet to find our girl," I tell her, my voice raw.

"She's okay. She called us on the way back to Kentucky. You said she told you she was okay."

"Yeah, but that fucker took her. I know our girl is strong, but..." I stop talking because the thought of him hurting my girl, of doing any fucking thing with her, is like a knife in the chest. It hurts too much to breathe.

"You know Kayden. We'll hear from her again very soon."

"And if we don't?"

"Then, I'll panic with you and the two of us will blow up the state of Virginia looking for her," she whispers kissing the side of my neck.

"God, I love you, Nicole."

"I love you too, Dragon. Forever," she murmurs and that one word makes me smile—just as it has all of these years I've had with her.

"Forever," I agree.

She shifts on the bed and I allow her to pull me back. The minute my head hits the pillow she pulls her body in close, her head on my chest and her leg thrown over me, curling into me. It's a move that has been familiar since the day we got together. It's a sensation that cuts me clear to the bone and makes me feel alive. It somehow soothes any ache I have. I knew all those years ago that Nicole was my home. She was the woman that I always wanted and never knew existed. Or, if it did exist, there was no way that she would find me worthy enough to have her. I was so full of myself back then, thinking I knew everything. I didn't know shit until a blonde with curves that went for days and a sassy mouth that alternated between driving me crazy and begging for more, stormed into my life barefoot.

"She's okay, Dragon."

"You can't know that, Mama."

"I do. I feel it. You said yourself that she didn't sound scared on the phone," she reminds me.

"She's my daughter she wouldn't show her fear."

"She's my daughter, too. Trust me, if she was scared you'd know it."

"I'm going to find her, Nicole."

"I know you will, Dragon."

"How can you be so sure?"

"Because you're you," she says simply, her faith in me absolute.

"You know when Bull told us the lengths he and Skye were going to just so he could knock her up, and how I told you I wanted another kid? Forget that shit."

"They've been together a lot of years now, Dragon. I don't think you should say he knocked her up. You should say they decided to have a baby together."

"Bullshit. They might have had to get medical help to make it work, but my boy made sure he fucked her extra, too—just to cover his bases. Therefore, he knocked her up."

"Have I ever told you that you're every woman's wet dream until you open your mouth?" she asks with a sigh.

"Once or twice, yeah," I respond, almost smiling, my fingers moving over her arm as we lie there in the dark. Neither of us speaks for a few minutes, each of us in our thoughts. I thought maybe she had drifted to sleep when she finally speaks.

"What's your next step?"

"Freak has called in some heavy markers. We're going to try to ping her cellphone through the satellites."

"How can you do that?"

"You know that shit is too technical for me, Woman. I just know it can be done."

"Yeah, but those markers... How would you even have those?"

"Men with power sometimes need shit done the old-fashioned way," I mutter, stretching to touch my lips to her temple. "Go to sleep, Mama. Tomorrow will be a busy day."

"What did Gunner say about this Chains?"

"He swears he's a good man. He says this guy is the reason his entire patrol team made it out of Kabul together."

"That's good right?"

"Depends," I say grudgingly.

"On what?"

"I've met a lot of men I might trust with the life of my men in battle. A lot of those same men I would kill if they got around my daughter."

"You can't kill this Chains until you know how your daughter feels about him, Dragon."

"The hell I can't. Kayden is too damn young, Nicole."

"She's not much younger than I was when I fell in love with a hard-headed biker who swept me off my feet," she murmurs, pressing a kiss against my skin.

"You got lucky."

"I can't argue with that. Love you, Honey," she tells me, sleep starting to thicken her voice.

"Night, Mama."

I lay there the rest of the night, holding my woman while she sleeps. I don't sleep. I don't think I'll be able to sleep until Kayden is back home where she belongs and this Chains fucker is ten feet underground.

28

KAYDEN

"Damn! Now that's a picture a man goes to war for," Chains says, his voice coming out like a hoarse, gritty sound that sends shivers over my body.

I look up at him, shading my eyes despite the fact I have my sunglasses on. God, he looks good today. His hair is rumpled from lying in bed and our lovemaking. He's wearing faded jeans, his feet are bare and he doesn't have a shirt on, so I can see all of his tattoos and scars. The scruff on his face is sexy and has a mixture of darker hair and gray in it. I have the strongest urge to kiss every inch of him. Chains is ruggedly handsome, definitely all man and the sight of him is enough to make my toes curl.

"I thought you were going to sleep the day away," I murmur.

Chain drops down on the small fishing dock that I'm lying on, immediately moving my head so that it rests in his lap. He leans down and kisses my forehead and we look out over the water.

"I had a woman who wore me the fuck out. I had to have time to recover," he says and my smile widens and I barely resist purring in satisfaction.

"Well, you are older. I hear recovery time can be a problem," I respond and he gives me a playful snarl, leaning down to bite on my neck and making me laugh.

"I don't want to leave here," I tell him once everything is quiet and the two of us are just looking out at the water."

"We don't have to, at least not anytime soon."

"If I don't call my Dad soon..." I trail off, not wanting to voice what will happen, but I know it and I'm pretty sure Chains knows it too.

"I'll take you into town tomorrow and you can call him."

"That can be dangerous," I warn him.

"Breathing can be dangerous, Baby Girl. We have to enjoy the time we have while we have it. When the time comes, your dad and I will work things out."

"That's what I'm afraid of," I mumble.

"What are you doing out here, besides working on your tan?" he asks, clearly done talking about my father. I let him get away with it, because I don't really want to talk about my father either.

"In case it has escaped your notice, Chains, I don't really need to work on my tan," I mutter, rolling my eyes at him—not that he can see me because I snatched my sunglasses from my car earlier. I checked my phone but it was dead. I didn't try to charge it, in fact I took the battery out of it. I have no idea if they can trace the damn thing, but I wouldn't put it past my dad.

"Oh, I noticed, Kayden. Or did you forget the way I licked every inch of you?"

"I seem to recall something along those lines," I respond, my body instantly becoming flushed with desire. Wetness pools against my panties and paints the insides of my thighs. I squirm uncomfortably. Chains being the cocky bastard he is, smirks at me. "What are you smiling about?" I mumble.

"My little virgin has turned into a hungry little cum slut," he says his voice amused, but I can hear the need in it too.

"I can't believe you just called me that," I grumble.

"Are you going to tell me I'm wrong?" he asks.

"Well, I mean, only *your* cum," I defend. "I don't think that makes me a slut."

"Baby Girl, I don't think you've got it yet, but you're not ever going to have another man's cum but mine. There's nothing wrong with wanting your man's cum all the time."

"Careful Chains, you're starting to sound cocky again."

"You like that too," he says and God help me, he's right.

"I'm kind of hungry," I mutter, deciding to change the subject.

"How about I grill us some burgers?" he asks, leaning down to kiss my forehead.

"Wow, you mean you can feed me instead of your ego? That's awesome."

"Just for that, Kayden you're going to stand outside on the deck while I grill the burgers."

"Gee, that's some harsh punishment there, Chains," I laugh getting up with him and his hand automatically rests on my back as he guides us back to the cabin.

"You have to do it naked," he says with a wink.

"Uh... what if someone sees us?"

"Doubtful, but if so then they'll know you're being fucked good," he responds, his voice matter-of-fact and completely casual. He opens up the door to the cabin and I step inside, still reeling from the shock. Chains is not joking. I think he even likes the idea of fucking me where people might see. I'm left trying to process that and wondering why the idea kind of turns me on...

29

CHAINS

"Chains, this is too much," Kayden says, looking down at the pendant I just slid around her neck. She holds the delicate diamond in her hand and looks back at me.

"You were admiring it in the window," I remind her.

We're standing in the jewelry store downtown. We ate lunch and were walking on the street. I discovered something about Kayden. She's not real big on going into shops, but she fucking loves looking in windows. It's the craziest thing. It does suit me however, because I hate shopping. Still, when she admired the pendant through the glass, I couldn't resist the urge to go in and buy it for her. I didn't expect it would freak her out.

"Well, yeah. It's pretty, but that doesn't mean you are supposed to buy it for me."

"I wanted to," I tell her, enjoying watching the way her finger is moving back and forth against the diamond.

"It's too much money," she argues again.

"Babe," I respond, shaking my head.

"I'm serious. It's too much money."

"It was just a couple hundred dollars, Kayden."

"You act like that's small change," she argues.

"Damn, women are supposed to love getting diamonds, They're not supposed to bust a man's balls."

"I'm not busting your balls. I'm just saying it's a lot. Sorry if I'm not like your other *women*," she mutters, looking down at the necklace and not at my face. She almost looks… embarrassed.

"Stop that," I tell her.

"What?" she asks, stubbornly, defiance flashing in her eyes when she finally looks at me.

"I've never bought another woman a diamond, Kayden. Not even my ex-wife."

Her face had started to go soft, and at the mention of my ex, I see shock. Christ, I haven't cared about a woman really, not like this, but even I'm smart enough to know you don't mention your ex around the woman you're slipping your dick into.

Or at least I should have been smart enough.

"You were *married*?"

"Kayden, I'm thirty. Is it that hard to believe I've been married?"

"Well I don't guess, I mean obviously it was a possibility. I just… I never really thought about it. What happened?"

"Came home early one day, found her sucking off someone I thought of as a friend, or at the very least someone I trusted enough to put my life in his hands."

"She cheated on you?"

"Yeah."

"With your friend?"

"Not sure I'd call him a friend now, Baby Girl."

"What a bitch," she huffs, clearly outraged, making me grin.

"That's one word for her," I respond, taking Kayden's hand in mine and walking down the sidewalk. "It's no big deal, Kayden. It's not like I was in love with her. I liked her, but I didn't shed a tear over her."

"I can't imagine you crying over any woman, Chains," she says, her fingers still on the diamond.

"I cried buckets over my mom."

"Your mom died?" she asks. She stops walking, turning to look at me, one hand still touching the diamond and one still joined with mine.

"A few years back. Cancer," I respond, and the sorrow I see on her face isn't make believe.

Kayden cares.

There's so much to love about Kayden, but the fact that she cares about me slides through me and settles in a way that I'm pretty sure it changes something elemental inside of me... something that I never knew was there. My hand tightens on hers as emotion passes through me that I'm mostly afraid to name.

"I'm sorry, baby," she replies, her voice gentle as she pulls her hand from the diamond I bought her and touches my face gently.

I memorize the look on her face. I never want to forget it, or the way she called me baby and the sweet tone in her voice when she did it.

I'm keeping her.

I don't know how I'm going to work it out, but I'm not letting her go. Her father will have to kill me. If he manages that, I'll go, but I'll die knowing that I held the best thing in this world in my hands and that for a moment, she belonged to me and me alone.

Kayden.

"I'm okay, Babe. Mom was suffering so much, it was good she passed on. You get to a point when you see them hurting so much and nothing you do will help, so you are ready to let them go, because you know your pain is better than watching them suffer."

Kayden goes up on the tips of her toes, stretching to kiss my lips. She doesn't deepen the kiss, she just makes it sweet and gentle. When she pulls back she doesn't leave. Instead she kisses my chest, right through my cut.

"What happened to your sisters?" she asks, while I'm still trying to deal with the sweetness of her and having trouble pushing my need for her away. I want her. I want her in ways that I don't understand.

"Kelly lives in Arkansas with her husband Deke who is in the Army. Liz is a teacher in Tennessee and lives in Mom's old house and Amy is in college at Lincoln Memorial in Tennessee."

"Do you get to see them often?"

"Not often, but enough. We talk on the phone some," I tell her. We start walking again and I pull her into the small variety store on the end of the walkway. I hate to do it, but I'll take her in to buy a throwaway phone so she can check in with her dad. He'll be on our tail soon, thanks to the money I dropped on my credit card. I'm dreading it, but I've never been one to run away from trouble. I usually face it head on, or in Kayden's case I tangle myself up in it so deep I'll never get free.

"What are we getting now?" she questions me. "I really think the diamond should tap out your shopping extravaganza for the day, Chains."

"My shopping extravaganza?" I laugh, shaking my head. "You're a damn nut, Kayden," I mutter.

"Yeah, but you like me," she says shyly and I pull on her hand so she'll look at me.

"That I do," I reply, and her eyes sparkle and those luscious full lips of hers curve into a smile.

"I like you too," she says so quietly I have to strain to hear her.

Yeah, I'm definitely tangled up in this woman. The strange thing about that is the deeper I get, the more I like it.

30

KAYDEN

"Well that went great," I mutter staring at the phone.

"You had to know it wouldn't, Kayden. Anyway that we played this your dad wasn't going to be happy having a roving grease monkey like me sniffing around his daughter. Taking you and carrying you out of your apartment screaming..." Chains shrugs not bothering to finish his thought.

"I have nosy neighbors," I mumble, flopping down on the couch.

Chains grabs me and pulls me so I'm sitting in his lap.

"Are you still hurting, Babe?" he asks, nuzzling my neck.

"I'm cramping a little." I sigh. "I'm the only woman in history who gets some stolen time with her... well whatever you are... and starts her period," I whine.

"Your man," Chains growls. "I'm your man, Kayden."

My heart skips a beat. I want to ask him how he feels about me. I want to ask him if he sees this going beyond just sleeping together. I haven't worked up my courage yet. I'm usually direct, but I'm actually terrified of Chains' answer because I think it might destroy me.

"You're missing the point here, Chains. We only have a limited amount of time together and I'm ruining it by getting a visit from Aunt Flo."

"First of all, you don't know how much time we have together. I'm not giving you up, Kayden." His words thrill me, and yet make me sad. I see the truth in his eyes, and I know he can see it in mine. My father will make this impossible. I'm hopeful I can talk him down, but that will take time and I'm scared that Chains will give up waiting for me and move on. When I look into Chains' eyes, suddenly a new resolve sweeps over me.

"I'm a grown woman," I announce, looking directly at Chains. He looks shocked for a minute and then his lips spread into a smile.

"Yeah, Babe. I think I got that the minute I sunk my dick into you—before, really."

"I get to decide when I sleep with someone and who I let into my pants."

"Now that is wrong."

"No, it's not," I argue.

"It sure as fuck is. I'm the only man you're letting in that sweet body of yours, Kayden. You want a cock, you get mine. You want tongue, it better damn well be mine. You want me to eat that sweet cunt while I'm fingering you, I'm down, any fucking time, because there's nothing I like better in this whole fucking world. But, it will only ever be me, Kayden. I was your first and Baby Girl, you better believe, I'm going to be your fucking last."

I listen to his words, a warmth filling me that I can't even begin to explain. That doesn't sound like he's just trying to fuck me out of his system...

"That sounds like you care," I whisper, only half realizing that I said the words out loud.

"Babe, I'm pissing off the biggest MC crew in this territory. A man doesn't just do that to get his rocks off. There's too much easy pussy for that shit."

"You're such a sweet talker," I mutter, shaking my head.

"You're too damn salty to like me if I was sweet."

"My point was that I'm just going to tell my father that I'm an adult and he will have to respect my choices and for some unknown reason, I'm choosing you."

"Not sure your father will accept that, but you have no idea how fucking good it feels to hear you say that you choose me."

"I'm sorry I'm ruining our night together," I sigh curling into him.

Chains puts his hand over my stomach, the heat that causes making the cramps just a little better.

"It's not ruined," he argues, rising off of the sofa, as if I weigh nothing.

"What are you doing now?" I ask him, breathing in the scent of him and burying my head in the curve of his neck.

"I'm going to take you and put you in a hot shower and let that ease your cramps and then..."

"Then?" I ask, pulling back to look at him.

"Then, I'm going to show you how a real man earns his medals in war."

"War medals?" I blink.

"A soldier isn't afraid to get a little blood on his sword, Babe. That's why he battles." He smiles a smile so dark and seductive my body quivers all over. He doesn't say anything else... but then, he doesn't need to.

31

DRAGON

"Tell me something good," I growl into the phone, needing some fucking good news here.

"I got shit from the phone Kayden used to call you, but our man Chains just used his credit card at a small jewelry shop in Norton, Virginia."

"Jewelry shop?"

"Dragon man, you may have to face the fact that Kayden might be just where she wants to be."

"Bullshit, you heard what the guy in the apartment next door said about her screaming that night."

"Dragon, how many times has Nicole screamed—"

"He handcuffed my baby girl to a damn steering wheel at a gas station, Freak. Does that sound like she was planning on staying around of her own free will?"

"Well, not exactly," he hedges.

"Exactly. I'm taking a cage and heading that way. I want Dancer, Bull, and at least three others with me."

"Dragon, maybe we should go at this quietly."

"When it's your kid involved in this shit, we'll talk. Until then, fuck off. Have the boys meet me in Manchester at the Stop and

Go. We'll head out from there, but they better not keep me waiting. I want to be in that damn jewelry store before noon."

"Got it. Maybe we—"

I hang up not letting him finish. Motherfucker thinks he's about to tell me what to do when it comes to my daughter, he better fucking think again.

"I'm going with you," Nicole says from behind me. I thought she was in the other room. I should have known she'd be listening for the phone.

"Nicole—"

"I'm going with you."

"You can't."

"Why in the hell not?"

"Did you forget Skye and Carrie are coming over?"

Her eyes narrow.

"I didn't invite them over."

"Bull said Skye has been depressed afraid she's too old to have a baby. I suggested they come over and you girls could plan a shower or whatever the shit it is you do."

"When did you suggest that to him?"

"A couple of days ago," I tell her, shrugging.

"Then, I'll just call and cancel."

"If Skye is already depressed, that could make it worse. She might feel like you want nothing to do with her."

"Dragon—"

"I'm just going to go get our daughter, Mama. That's it. I can move quicker without you and have her home by nightfall."

"You promise you won't do anything stupid?"

"I promise."

"I don't believe you."

I smile at her, even if I don't feel like it.

"I'll bring her home, Mama."

"And not kill anyone?"

"Nicole," I growl, my patience wearing thin.

"Promise me you won't kill him, Dragon. At least until we hear what Kayden has to say."

"Fucking hell," I mutter.

"If you don't promise, I'm going with you."

"Fine. I won't kill the bastard—*yet.*"

"Dragon—"

"That's as good as you're going to get from me, Mama. Take it or leave it."

"Fine. Be careful. I don't know why, but I'd miss your bull-headed ass if I lost you."

"Love you, Nicole," I tell her giving her a quick kiss. I am almost out the door when she calls out.

"And Dragon?"

I stop and turn and look at her. Jesus she's still beautiful, even after all this time. I don't know what I ever did to deserve her light in my life, but just thinking about the days before she came to Kentucky is painful.

"Yeah, Mama?"

"Don't think I don't know why you invited Skye and Carrie over. You're going to be paying for that one."

"Bye, Nicole," I mutter, shaking my head and walking on out of the house.

I'm in my SUV and merging onto the main road before I take out my phone.

"I'm suiting up now, Dragon. I'm meeting Dancer and Nailer at the club," Bull says the second he answers.

"Good. I need you to tell Skye that Nicole invited her and Carrie over today to discuss a baby shower."

"I... Boss, Skye doesn't like that shit..."

"She does now," I mutter. "Oh and tell her you were supposed to tell her that a couple of days ago and forgot."

"Jesus, Boss. You're going to get me locked out of my pussy for weeks."

"When we get off the phone, tell Dancer the same shit," I

respond, not really caring if Bull has to go without. If he can't take control of his woman, he deserves blue balls.

"Will do," he mumbles and I hang up, tossing my phone into the passenger seat.

I'm going to go find my girl and then I'm going to show this Chains fucker exactly what happens when he tries to hold my girl against her will.

Cuffing her to a motherfucking steering wheel.

I saw the video surveillance at that damn gas station myself. I may have promised Nicole I wouldn't kill him right away, but that's only because I'm going to enjoy dragging him slowly toward his death.

That's for damn sure.

32

CHAINS

"What in the hell are you doing?"

"I..." For a second, she looks trapped—which she is. Then, she gets that sassy look on her face, the one that never fails to make my dick go hard. "I thought you were sleeping," she huffs.

"I was and pretty damn good, too. Then, I found my arms empty instead of holding my woman. So, I repeat, what in the hell are you doing?"

She narrows her eyes at me.

"I had to pee!"

I cock my eyebrow up at her response, because we both know she's lying. Then I lean up against the wall, folding my arms at my chest like I haven't got a care in the world.

"Were you planning on pissing on the couch? Or going outside and squatting on the deck?"

"What?" she asks, her nose scrunched up.

"Well you're not in the bathroom, so I can only assume you are in here to do the deed here. So have at it."

"I..."

"I'm just going to stand here and watch the show."

"I can't pee in front of you," she mumbles.

"You are the single most stubborn female I've ever been around."

"Chains—"

"We both know you're not here to take a piss. So, I'm going to repeat my question, what in the hell are you doing, Kayden?"

"I'm looking for the car keys," she sighs.

"What for?"

"I… I need to get home, Chains. I need to try and get ahead of my father. If not, this could end really badly."

"What happened to you being a grown woman and your father would just have to accept your choices?" I ask, fighting a smile, because I can tell she's torn up over this.

"I am and he will… it's just it may take a lot to talk him down. If you think I'm stubborn, Chains, I'm nothing compared to my father. He wrote the damn book on stubborn."

"I told you I'll deal with your father when the time comes. We'll head back to Kentucky next week. I just want more time alone with you before all of the bullshit."

"Chains, my father is probably on his way here—or already here. You did use a credit card yesterday," she reminds me, her fingers going to the diamond I bought her. I wasn't sure she would catch that, but this just proves she's sharp as a damn tack.

"They might be in town, but no one knows us and this place sure as hell isn't on the radar. We're good here."

"The longer we wait, the worse it will be, Chains," she says, biting down on her lip in worry.

I release an aggravated breath, because I'm not ready to give up our time together—not yet. She is right, however. I didn't realize it was bothering her so much and I really don't want her stressing over this shit.

"Fine. We'll head back in the morning."

"Really?" she asks, her eyes going wide with shock.

"Yes, really. I told you, Kayden. I'm not giving you up. If it takes me heading back to Kentucky early and dealing with your father, so be it."

"It's not going to be easy," she warns me, walking the few steps between us, to stand in front of me.

"I didn't figure it would be," I tell her, immediately taking her in my arms.

"I could love you, Chains," she whispers, leaning against me and kissing my chest.

"You better learn to, because I told you, I'm not letting you go."

"Will you learn to love me?" she asks.

"Probably, but you sure as hell are going to be a pain in my ass."

"You're such a jerk," she mumbles.

"But, I'm your jerk," I tell her, grinning down at her.

"There is that," she laughs.

"Come on, Woman. I'll let you take me into the bedroom and make it up to me for sneaking out of our bed."

"Gee, that's so nice of you."

"I thought so," I tell her as we walk.

"How am I supposed to make it up to you?"

I stop to look at her and let my finger move over her lip.

"We'll figure something out," I tell her, visions of her swallowing my cock down that sweet little throat of hers flashing through my mind.

She laughs, knowing what I'm thinking. But, she must want it just as bad, because she jogs into the bedroom leaving me to follow behind her.

Yeah... I could definitely love her...

33

KAYDEN

When Chains finally gets to the bedroom, I'm sitting on the side of the bed. I'm nervous, still not sure I should have given in. Chains said we'd go back tomorrow and that's going to have to be enough. Besides, if I'm honest, I want one more day with him. I want to hide away from the world, just the two of us and I don't want to think about the chaos my father might try to cause. I can only hope that once he sees how serious I am, how I'm not going to give Chains up, he'll back off. If that doesn't work, I'll beg Mom to help me. She's the only one that's ever been able to get him to do anything.

With my mind made up and the decision made, I decide to focus on the one thing I can control at the moment and that's making my man so happy that he might think I'm worth the shit my father might put him through, when we get back.

"Shouldn't you be on your knees, waiting for your man?" Chains—the cocky bastard—asks. I'd complain, but I like him being cocky, for some unknown reason, it even makes me happy.

"Sit down beside me first," I tell him.

He doesn't question me further, he just sits down and I'm so grateful that I turn and kiss him. It's not a deep kiss, or rather, it wasn't meant to be. But Chains takes over and the kiss gets heated and sweet, making my entire body shiver in anticipation.

"Have I told you that you really know how to kiss, Chains?"

"Maybe once or twice. I could say the same about you, but that makes me think of all the men you might have kissed before me and then, instead of having your sweet lips wrapped around my cock, I'll be out hunting motherfuckers I need to kill for trying to touch what's mine."

"You're a little crazy," I laugh.

"About you, definitely," he growls.

Maybe it's a throwaway compliment, something he doesn't even realize he's saying, but the words cause my heart to flutter weirdly in my chest. I should probably stop fighting the truth, that Chains has worked his way inside my heart. I don't know how it happened.

I slide down to my knees in front of him. My nerves are getting the better of me, but I ignore them—or at least try too.

"I'm new at this, so you'll need to be patient," I warn him as I wrap my hand around his thick shaft. His cock is so hot that it surprises me. How can something be so warm when it's been swinging out freestyle? It's not like this cabin is heated.

Then, all thought leaves me as I stroke him and can feel the power inside of him, as my hand moves over him. He's hard yet pliable, stiff yet moves in exactly the way I want him too.

"Baby, your hand on my cock is better than anything I've ever felt. I'm a simple man. If you're giving my dick attention, it's all good," he says, his voice coarse and hungry and it moves over me like a physical praise.

This is mine.

Chains is mine. He might be possessive over me, but it's definitely a two-way street and there's a freedom in knowing that.

As I stroke him a couple of times, I just watch my hand move. It's beautiful in the simplicity of it. I should be the one vulnerable, but I'm not. I hold all the power over this strong, alpha male.

I stroke him again, my hand moving slowly but steady and as I reach the tip of his shaft, I twist lightly and squeeze.

"Fuck," he hisses and my gaze drags away from his cock to see his face. I'm afraid I might have done something wrong, but all I see is pleasure.

This time, as I give an upward stroke, my thumb moves along a large, bulging vein on the underside of his cock. It seems to pulsate with my touch. I don't know if it's right or wrong, but Chains said as long as I was giving him attention and playing with his cock, it was all good. I let that embolden me and I flatten my tongue out and lick along its path, not stopping until I reach his tip. I can taste his precum on the head and I curl my tongue against the source seeking more. My other hand going to rub against his balls, as I find that I want to touch every beautiful inch of him.

"That's it, Baby," he praises. "Get my cock nice and wet. Let me fuck that sweet mouth of yours," he adds.

Jesus, those words alone cause a gush of wetness to coat my thighs. I'm supposed to make him come, but I have no doubts that this could make me come too, the pleasure is that intense.

"Like this?" I whisper, my voice not even recognizable to my own ears.

I hold his cock as steady as I can, considering my hand is shaking, then, I suck just the tip of him in my mouth, and my tongue slides against the head, loving the feel of it. Next, I suck on it, applying pressure almost as fierce as the way I'm holding his shaft. I look up at him to see his reaction. Chains' eyes are closed, but there's no denying the pleasure that's taken over his expression.

Pleasure that I've given him.

That thought spurs me on, and I slide my mouth down, taking in more of his cock, working him in my mouth until I can barely breathe. He's at the back of my throat, but there's still more of him. I want to take it all, but I'm not sure it's possible.

"Relax that throat baby, breathe through your nose and take me deeper," Chains instructs, but he doesn't sound cocky now. No, now it's almost as if he's begging. There's so much raw need in his voice that it soothes me, makes me feel beautiful and makes me want to give him so much pleasure that he gets completely lost.

I do as he asked, and I fight my gag reflex as his hard, stiff cock slides deeper, my mouth stretched around it. I make it to where my lips are against the little nest of curled hair at his base.

"Oh fuck. Oh yeah... God, woman," Chains growls from above me. I moan because it feels so good and I'm so wet, my nipples are tingling, my body craving him. I don't want to stop. I want to make him come. I want to make Chains lose control.

I slide off of his cock, and then immediately take him back in. His hands tighten in my hair as he begins fucking me—fucking my mouth, just like he said he wanted.

And it's definitely what I want.

I never want him to stop...

34

CHAINS

My balls are so tight, I know I'm going to blow; I can't stop it. Kayden is gorgeous, her mouth a perfect fucking heaven and she holds my cock tight, sucking so hard that it feels like I might die from the fucking pleasure.

"That's it, Baby, suck it down," I groan, my thumb brushing against her temple and I push her hair over her shoulder so I can watch her take every damn inch.

She hums around my cock, the vibration sending pleasure through my body. She's gobbling down every fucking inch she can, her hand tight around the base, as she takes complete control. I don't normally allow that. I usually like to be in control, but I let her have her way, because it's fucking beautiful and nothing has felt better in my life.

She pulls me out of her mouth, her lips slick with my pre-cum. One small pearl strand, sliding from the corner. I take my thumb, catching it and pushing it back into her mouth, our gazes locked.

"Are you going to come for me, Chains?" she asks, literally moaning the question.

"Take the shirt off, Kayden," I order her, my voice so thick with desire it's almost unrecognizable. In response, she squeezes my cock tightly. I growl and I swear my fucking legs go weak it feels so good.

"I don't want to let you go," she argues.

"Do it."

I see it in her eyes and know she's going to fight me before she even makes a move. Her mouth goes back down on my cock, thinking to deny me of what I want—*what I need.* I wrap my fingers in her hair and pull her off, before I let the pleasure talk me out of it.

"Take off your fucking shirt, Kayden."

"Chains," she complains, her voice is this sweet little whine that makes my dick jerk.

"I want that fucking shirt off. I'm going to blow soon and when I do, I'm coming all over that mouth and those pretty tits of yours. I want to see my cum all over that beautiful dark skin and then you and I are going to rub my cum into you, so you're covered in my scent. I want to make sure you're marked as mine in a way that only we will know, but in a way that we'll never forget. Now, I'm only going to say it one more time, Kayden. Take off the fucking shirt."

Her eyes go round, her mouth opening in surprise as she takes in my words. Then she completely lets go of my cock and whips the shirt off quickly throwing it on the floor beside her.

"Good girl. Now, open wide and flatten out that wicked little tongue for me," I tell her, starting to stroke my own cock, my gaze locked on hers. She licks her lips, but doesn't argue. Instead, she does exactly as I ask. "I like it when you do as I ask, Baby."

"Don't get used to it," she says with a smirk and it makes me smile.

"Hold those tits out for me. Offer yourself up to me, Kayden."

Again, she does as I ask. To reward her, I bend down and suck one of those plump nipples into my mouth, biting it just hard enough to make her body quiver in reaction. I love watching that and the way her eyes close in pleasure, without her saying a word. When she opens them back up they're dark, liquid pools of hunger. Kayden has the most beautiful eyes I've ever seen in my life. Fuck that, everything about her is perfect, she's beyond compare.

"Do it, Chains," she urges me. "Give me your cum, mark me," she says and the way she says it, along with the look on her face, almost makes it like she's daring me. I start jacking my cock slowly. I lay the head of my cock against her tongue, pumping him so slow I groan out. I squeeze the head, forcing a large drop of cum to drizzle out against her tongue. I pull back to watch her curl her tongue up and swallow it down, her face satisfied and greedy. It looks so fucking good that I pump my cock again, but this time I move it around her lips, making them shine with my cum.

"Are you going to play around all day, or give me what we both want," she challenges.

I look at her, feeling emotion that is completely foreign to me and something I've never felt before. Christ, somehow this woman grabbed me by the balls when I wasn't looking and now...

She fucking owns me.

Is that love?

It feels like more than that. I loved my mom. I loved my sisters. Fuck, you love a dog. Kayden possesses me. I'm not letting her go, I don't think I could continue to survive without her and suddenly I realize the truth. I was only surviving until she came into my life.

"You belong to me," I tell her, my voice guttural and raw.

"Chains..."

"You fucking belong to me Kayden. You're not leaving me. If this shit goes south and you're forced to choose between me and staying in Kentucky and your mom and dad, you'll choose me."

"Chains, Honey..."

"Admit it, Kayden."

I need the fucking words from her. Years of service and facing wars, years of drifting and not once—not one damn time have I felt the fear I feel inside right now. I don't want to lose her...

I can't.

"I'm not leaving you," she says, her hands moving to my thighs, her nails digging in, giving just a small sting of pain. I like that she does that, I like the way it grounds me to this moment, focuses my attention to her every movement, her every expression. Her eyes stay locked on mine, as her tongue flattens out and licks the underside of my cock like a fucking ice cream cone, from the tip to the root and back again. She swallows down another strand of cum and that's the minute I know I can't hold back any more. I start pumping my cock harder, getting ready to cover her sweet body.

"Kayden," I gasp as I feel my body flush with heat and I know I'm getting ready to come. Her name on my lips, her beauty before me, her eyes locked on me... Jesus, she's everything. I move my gaze down to her tits as she holds them out to me again, offering them to me. My hand trembles as I jack my cock, my orgasm getting closer.

"I'd choose you, Chains," she whispers and I jerk my attention back to her face, her words surprising me. "I'd chose you every time, Honey," she says and as I look at her face, those words echoing in my ears, there's no way I can doubt her. She means everything she's saying.

"Kayden," I groan, needing to come, but hating that this is almost over.

"I love you, Chains," she whispers and I need to give the words back to her. I want to, but all I can do is cry out her name as my cum jets out splashing against her body. I empty myself on her, jet after jet, after jet. Giving her everything, because the simple truth is she owns me. I've never felt like this about someone else and I know instinctively I never will again. I want to tell her that as I spend the last of my cum, letting it drop down her chin and run down her neck. I bring my hand to her neck and run my fingers over it, rubbing my essence into her body. She doesn't blink, her hand caps over mine and we rub it in together, our gazes locked on one another. It feels important, it feels like we're completely together, the two of us... *one.*

There was a time I would have laughed at that shit, but looking at her beautiful face, feeling what I'm feeling and seeing the same emotion on her... I can't deny it.

It's time.

Time to give her the words I never thought I would give any woman, especially after my fucked-up history with my ex-wife.

"Kayden," I start, my voice low and hoarse, my breathing ragged.

Before I can get the rest of the words out there's a crashing noise from the other room. My body tenses for fucking attack. I look around for my gun, but it and my cut are on the other side of the room. Before I can spring into action, the door to the bedroom is kicked open, slamming against the wall so powerfully that it breaks off the hinge and slams hard against the wall. I cover Kayden pulling her into my body, not wanting them to see her. I recognize the men. It looks like Dragon somehow found the cabin.

"What the fuck?" the large man holding the gun aimed at my head yells.

It looks like I just met Kayden's father.

35

KAYDEN

Every nightmare I've ever had pales in comparison to what I'm feeling and experiencing right now.

"Fuck," I hear Chains hiss.

"Chains," I whisper against his ear, because he has me plastered to him, shielding me from my father and his men.

I allow myself a moment of weakness, hiding my face in the chest of the man I love and wonder how on earth I'm going to get us out of this.

"Kayden get the fuck away from him," Daddy yells, in a tone I don't think I've ever heard from him.

Chains reaches down and finds his shirt that I was wearing, grabs it and starts trying to cover me with it.

"Get those damn men out of here and let her cover up," Chains growls. There's so much anger in his voice that I know him and Dad are going to go at each other hard. My stomach flips and somersaults. This is going to be bad... so bad. I should have left earlier when I had a chance. I should have tried to get in front of this somehow. I knew Dad would blow up, but I don't think I knew how bad it was going to be. Then again, there was no way to guess the amount of fury coming off of my father. All at once,

Chains goes down, hitting the ground hard. I scream, trying to lean over him. I bring my hand to the side of his head, above his ear. I think I scream when my fingers touch blood. I look up to see my father, standing there, fury coming off of him in waves, holding his gun so the butt of it is facing me and it has blood on it.

"You pistol whipped him!" I cry, anger building up in me and overtaking my panic. "Chains, oh God, Baby! Are you okay?" I lean down trying to wake him. His eyes open, but they look foggy, definitely not focused.

"Get the fuck away from him, Kayden!" Dad yells.

"I'm... okay," Chains says, sluggishly. He rises back up, shaking his head.

"You might be okay right now, but soon you won't be," Dad says. "Soon, there won't be nothing but pieces of you motherfucker," he adds, cocking his gun and pressing it right against Chains' head.

"Don't do this here man. Let Kayden leave," Chains says and that's when the fear truly grabs hold of my heart.

"No! Dad! Stop this! I love him! You can't hurt him."

"Get the hell away from him and go shower, Kayden."

"No!"

"You want my men to see what a whore this scum has turned you into?" Dad growls.

His words pierce me and rob me of air as much as if he had slapped me. I don't get a chance to respond, though. Because suddenly there's an unholy noise that reminds me of a wounded bear. Then, a wounded Chains, launches himself at my father. He obviously doesn't care he's completely naked. He's going after him and from the way he sounds he's intent on hurting him.

"No one calls Kayden a whore. I'll kill you!" Chains screams.

He catapults his body up, but the hit he took has bothered him. I can tell by the way he weaves. He tackles Dad, wrestling him down. The gun goes off and I scream, just as Uncle Bull's arms wrap around me and he drags me away, pulling me off the ground.

The echo of the gun vibrates in my ear and I fight to see what happened as Dad's men circle around him and Chains, blocking my view completely.

36

DRAGON

I hit the fucker again with the butt of my gun. He's bleeding, but I'm pretty fucking sure it just nicked him. I won't fucking cry if he bleeds out though. I can tell Nicole he jumped me and took the decision out of my hands. I kick the asshole to see if he moves.

"Trying to turn my daughter into your fucking whore? You think you can come into my territory and mess with my fucking family? I'm going to crush you like the piss ant you are. I'll cut you up in so many fucking pieces the crows will get dizzy trying to collect them all," I yell.

"Daddy, don't. I love him!" Kayden cries.

Chains doesn't say a fucking thing, even as I'm kicking him over and over. He's out of it. I hope the asshole is dead, but I doubt he makes it that easy for me. My men part and there's my girl pulling against Bull's hold. She's crying, trying to get to the bastard on the floor. Her gaze moves up to mine and she locks on my face. I look over to see if she's hurt and what I see makes my stomach turn. My baby girl covered in some fuckers spunk.

"Jesus Christ. What has he done to you, Kayden?"

"I love him! Oh God, did you shoot him? *Is he dead!?!?!?!*" she cries, trying to tear out of Bull's arms.

"I hope the fucker is, but if he's not, I'll make sure he's that way before I'm done," I tell her. "Go get in the shower and clean up before I take you back to your mother."

"I'm not going anywhere. Call an ambulance for Chains, now!"

"The only thing I'd call for Chains is a hearse, but he won't need that either. I'll let the crows eat on him."

"You will not! You will get him help now or so help me God, Daddy, I will never forgive you."

"I can live with that. Now go get your ass in the shower."

"No! Call an ambulance!"

"Bull, go throw her in the shower."

"Uh... Boss..."

"Jesus," I growl when it's clear Bull isn't going to do as I ordered. I step over the fuck-head bleeding on the floor and walk to my daughter. Her body goes solid as I approach her.

"If you so much as touch me, I'll make sure you regret it," she threatens, her voice quiet and definitely filled with anger and hate.

I ignore her and take her out of Bull's arms. I don't move fast enough because her leg moves back and then moves up with all the force she can and knees me in the balls.

Motherfucker!

That hurts like hell. For a minute I think I might throw up and make a fool of myself. I remain standing, but it's a close thing. I toss Kayden over my shoulder and take her, kicking and screaming, into the attached bathroom.

"If you don't get him help right now, Dad, so help me God, I will never forgive you!"

I ignore her, turning the water up as hot as it will go. When I'm sure it's hot, but won't peel her hide, I let her slide down onto the tiled shower floor. She sputters as the water hits her face.

"Wash that crap off of you. The last thing I need to be reminded of is how my daughter acted like a fucking prostitute for a man that's too damn old for her—not to mention a fucker who handcuffed her to a damn steering wheel. Jesus, Kayden, what were you thinking?"

"I was thinking that I'm in love with Chains and we're going to be together for the rest of our lives! You'll just have to get used to it," she declares.

"Let me clear this up for you, he's not going to be alive, so that declaration means shit to me. Now shower so I can get your ass home to your mother."

"I hate you!" she yells.

I push her back under the spray so some of that shit will leave her body. It's mostly dried on her at this point, but you can definitely tell the fucker bathed her in it. I'm going to throw a fucking party once I cut off his dick and feed it to him.

"Get your ass under the water and you can hate me back in Kentucky."

"I need you to promise me you won't hurt Chains anymore. I love him, Daddy."

"We can stand here and argue about it if you want, Kayden, but that fucker in there is bleeding out and every second you delay, you're just making my job easier. We're not leaving this place until you get his damn shit off your face and every minute I'm forced to stare at it just makes me want to kill him even more."

"I'm never going to forgive you, Daddy. Never," she yells. I close the bathroom door and ignore her.

Fuck it. I'm going to enjoy killing that son of a bitch, if for no other reason than just because of the shit I'm going through with Kayden. Hell, and I'm sure Nicole will give me just as much hell.

It's too damn bad I can't kill this motherfucker twice...

37

CHAINS

"My wife says I can't kill you."

"And that's why I'm still alive?" I ask, wiping my busted lip off with the back of my hand. My breath is coming out in ragged spurts. I'm pretty sure I have a couple of cracked ribs. My eyes are swollen, and I can barely see out of one of them. My body is sore from fighting with the twisted motherfucker sitting across from me, but that's it. Well, unless you count the bullet hole in my shoulder, but that was more from wrestling over the gun. I actually get the feeling he's pulling his punches somewhat with me. Since I'm still fucking healing from the shot and sore as hell, I appreciate that fact more than I should, I guess.

"Part of it," he says with a shrug like he doesn't give a fuck and I guess he doesn't.

"Guess I don't need to ask who wears the pants in the family."

"Fuck you. I just happen to like my woman's pussy. If I kill you, she could decide not to give it to me. That wouldn't work for me, so you're still breathing. Don't worry, I'll probably kill you soon," he says, sounding bored.

"How's Kayden?"

"None of your fucking business."

"Just tell me if she's okay."

"You want to tell me why you thought you could come into my town and lay your fucking hands on my daughter? I know you're a fucking nomad, but you know how this shit works. You know to respect the fucking order of things. My daughter is fucking off limits, especially to a piece of shit like you. She's too good for the likes of you. Hell, she's too good for any of us."

"On that, we can agree. Kayden deserves a fuck of a lot more than me," I mumble, wishing I could see her, if only one more time. I know she's blaming herself and I don't want that. I underestimated Dragon and because of that, I fucked all this up. I should have done things differently and I sure as hell should have protected Kayden better.

"It's good you know that. Does that mean if I let you go, you're going to get the fuck out of Kentucky?"

"If that's what you want, man, you might as well kill me. I'm never giving Kayden up."

"That's some strong words for a man in chains at the moment," he says leaning back in his chair and taking a long pull from his beer.

"Don't suppose I can have one of those?" I mutter, eyeing his bottle.

"Sure," he says, surprising me.

He nods over to his man, Dancer, who frowns at him but brings me a beer out of a small fridge. He hands it to Dragon, frowning at him. Dragon puts it down at my feet.

I know it's impossible, but I still try reaching down to grab the damn thing. The chains around my wrists pull, but there's no way I can reach the shit.

"You're a fucking asshole," I mutter, leaning back against the wall.

"I thought the chains were a poetic touch," he smirks finishing off his bottle.

"My woman must have taken after her mother," I mutter,

lying through my fucking teeth. I'm starting to see why she's so damn stubborn.

"She's not your woman, motherfucker. She's *my* daughter."

"If I make it out of this, she's *my* woman. You need to get used to that, because I'm not a fucking kid that's going to walk away from the best thing that's ever happened to me. I'm keeping her. You got a problem with that, you might as well go ahead and kill me so I don't have to hear your damn voice constantly."

"You're either brave or the stupidest son of a bitch I've ever met in my life. Look around you asshole. Do you think I'm playing a game here?"

I don't say anything. Instead, I use my bare feet, curling them on each side of the bottle and lift the fucking thing up high enough the chains on my wrists let me grab it. It hurts like hell, because my body has been battered. Pain shoots through my damn shoulder, but the pain is more than worth it as my hands grab the beer and I take a long, cold swig.

Dragon surprises me by laughing. I look over at him out of the corner of my good eye.

"Damn, Chains. I could almost like you if you hadn't fucked with my daughter."

"I didn't fuck *with* your daughter. I *fucked* her and I plan on doing it again."

"And just like that I want to kill you. You son of a bitch, my daughter is not some girl you can make a whore out of," he growls.

"If you call my woman that one more time, I don't care if Kayden loves you, Dragon, I will find a way to fucking kill you. I was the first man between Kayden's legs and I'll be the fucking last."

Dragon looks at me, but I'm done. He's said that shit way too much about her. He's her father, he should know what a special woman she is. He should cherish it.

"Enjoy your beer, Chains. It may be your last one," he says, not saying anything else. He gets up, slaps me on the shoulder, and walks away, leaving me alone.

And confusing the fucking hell out of me.

38

DRAGON

"Dragon man, you're fucking up," Dancer says the minute I walk in the door. Bull, doesn't say anything, but he nods his head in agreement.

They're sitting in chairs that are placed in front of the glass wall, watching Chains. It's a two-way mirrored room. He can't see us, but we definitely can see him. That means, they've seen me talk to him, they hear what he says when we talk and I know they like him... I know because they've told me.

Shit, I think I kind of like him.

"If it was Jazz he was fucking around with, I don't think you'd be singing that damn tune," I mutter, leaning up against the wall, watching Chains and trying to figure out what in the fuck I'm doing. Kayden's not talking to me, Nicole is barely giving me the time of day and something has to give soon. Hell, it's getting to where I dread going home.

"Shit, if it was Jazz, I'd be celebrating," Dancer says. "I swear to fuck that girl is going to kill me off. How a kid that was as sweet as she was, could turn into such a ..."

"Spoiled brat?" Bull adds helpfully.

"Fuck you," Dancer mutters, but he sure as hell doesn't deny it. Then again, he couldn't. Jazz is spoiled and everyone fucking knows it. She's a good kid, but she definitely thinks the world owes her. Dance and Carrie spoiled her for sure, but no more than the rest of us did our kids. I'm not sure what in the fuck happened with Jazz, so I don't say anything—mostly, because there is nothing to say.

Instead, I sigh and rub the back of my neck, studying the man I should hate, but grudgingly like. The worst thing about him, is I think he cares for my girl. Hell, I can even understand why he kidnapped her and chained her to the steering wheel. If Nicole had pulled her shit way back when, I would have done the same thing, because I sure as hell wouldn't have given her up.

Still, I can't let Chains kidnap my daughter, no matter what's going on, and get away with it. He needs to learn his lesson and I need to make sure others see it. I have to draw a line in the damn sand. This is something I never thought I'd have to deal with, but Chains and Kayden forced my hand, so I have to.

And I have to do it quick, because Kayden is getting too fucking pissed at me and with each hour that goes by, Nicole is talking to me less and less...

Kayden always swore she'd never end up with a biker. I love my way of life, but I was relieved when Kayden told me that. Mostly because I didn't want to have to kill one of my own if they made a play for her.

She's my little girl. I want her to have the world. I want her to be happy.

Christ, I just didn't want to have to deal with this shit in general. She's so fucking young, I thought I had more time. I thought Kayden would take her time before finding the man she wanted to settle down with.

I'm just not fucking prepared...

And what's more... I'm not sure I ever will be...

39

NICOLE

"Are you going to keep giving me the silent treatment?" Dragon snarls as he gets in bed.

"I don't know who told you that you could sleep in here, but either you go to the guest room, or I will."

"I'm not fucking going to sleep in the guest room. You and I don't sleep apart, Nicole."

"We do when you're being an idiot, Dragon. Now, which one of us is going to the guest room? But, I'm warning you, if you make me give up my bed because you're too fucking selfish to sleep in another room, I'm packing my damn bags and going to stay with Dani for a few days."

"The fuck you are," he growls, sitting up in bed. "Christ, I don't know why in the hell you have to be so fucking unreasonable about this shit."

"Unreasonable? You're lucky I'm letting you stay in the house at all after what you called our baby girl," I cry, reaching over and turning the light on.

"I think I liked it better when you gave me the silent treatment, woman."

"Too damn bad. Now are you leaving or not?"

"Fuck no, I'm not leaving."

"Fine, then I am," I mumble, moving out of bed to find my robe.

"You take one step out of this room Nicole, and I will spank your ass so hard that you won't sit down for a week."

"Dragon, if you don't back down from this mess and make our daughter happy, you won't see my ass again."

"What the fuck?"

I sigh, because I know he thinks I meant I would move out. Really, I only meant no sex. I'd explain, but that'd probably make him worse.

"You called our daughter a whore," I tell him, my voice sounding raw because of the pain inside of me. Kayden was heartbroken for many reasons, but the fact her father—the father she has always adored—could talk to her like that, broke something inside of her.

"You weren't there. You didn't see..."

Dragon stops talking. He sits up, throwing his feet off the side of the bed and rubbing the back of his head in frustration. It's something I've seen often over the years. When it happens I usually move in behind him, hold him close and tell him how much I love him. I won't be doing that tonight. I know he's hurting, and I know he feels backed into a corner. The problem is that he has us all backed into the same corner and no one can back down. It's all on him.

"You walked in on a private moment."

"She's our *daughter*, Nicole," he snarls, grabbing his cell off the nightstand and hurling it against the wall so that it shatters into a thousand pieces.

"She is and you had her all to yourself for almost nineteen years, Dragon. She's not a little baby anymore."

"She's my baby damn it. I was there when she took her first breath. I changed her fucking diapers. I held her hand when she lost her cat Tassels. I was there through it all damn it."

God. I can't stop from walking to him, because I can hear the pain in his voice. My man has few weaknesses, unless you know where to look.

I sit down on the bed beside him and hug up against him. His arm comes out immediately and holds me.

"You'll always be there for her, Dragon. But, she loves this Chains and everything I hear tells me that he's a good man. You need to let her grow up now."

"Kayden is blinded, you can't trust what she says. She barely knows this asshole."

"I didn't hear it from her."

"Who?" he grumbles.

"Dancer, Gunner, Bull, Nailer—"

"Fucking men talk more than a bunch of old women in a nursing home."

"Doesn't change the facts. What's more is, I think *you* like him."

"He handcuffed my daughter—"

"He didn't do anything you wouldn't have done to me. Has it been so long ago that you've forgotten, Dragon?"

"I haven't forgotten anything, Mama."

"You're going to have to let him go. You need to give them a chance."

"He's a fucking nomad. I don't want my daughter living from place to place with no roots. She deserves more than that. She *wanted* more than that, Nicole."

"How do you know he won't give it to her? You were just going to fuck me until you got tired of me, remember? That's not exactly how it turned out."

"I didn't know you had a voodoo pussy."

"Not this again," I respond, shaking my head.

"I'm tellin' you, it needs a fucking warning label. It draws a dick in and you never want to leave it."

I roll my eyes at him, but I'm rewarded when he smiles.

"You need to let him go, Dragon. Let Kayden have a chance for happiness. She'll always be your little girl."

"What if the fucker hurts her, Nicole?"

"Like you did? You called our baby a whore, Dragon. I get that you were mad and you had every right to be. Kayden knew we'd be upset, she should have handled it all differently, from the moment we thought she was abducted. But, you broke her heart. She loves you so much."

"I didn't mean it. It was the shock. I walked in and seen... I should have cut his dick off and fed it to him for that shit. He made her into—"

"If you say it, so help me Dragon there won't be any way for you to save yourself with me," I warn him.

"I'm just saying, that shit..."

"You fucked me almost from the moment we first met and had me screaming out for more, while everyone in the next room heard us, Dragon."

"Those were some good times, Mama."

"You made the whole club leave the room to fuck me when you saw my tattoo. Did those times make me a whore?" I ask, pressing my case and doing my best to hide my smile, because they were good times. Ones we still recreate from time to time. We might be older, but we sure as hell aren't dead yet.

"I'll apologize," he mutters.

"And you'll let Chains go?"

"Eventually."

"Dragon!"

"Damn it, Mama, I can't give in all at once. How in the fuck is that going to look to my men?"

"You have a choice, Dragon. You can man up here, and make our little girl happy again..." I respond, standing up and untying my robe.

"Or?" he asks, his hands tunneling under my robe to hold onto my hips.

"Or you can keep fucking up and none of this will be yours for a *very* long time," I finally answer, letting the robe fall down to the floor.

"You threatening to lock me out of your pussy, Mama?"

"Yeah, I am."

"That's cold, Mama."

"Make it right, Dragon. I can promise you that you won't regret it." I gasp the last word out because Dragon pulls me down onto his lap and suddenly we're skin against skin, his hard cock pushing up against my center, the lips of my pussy parting for him, allowing him to slide between them.

"If he fucks up, can I kill him then?" Dragon asks, almost hopeful as he slides me back and forth on his shaft. I'm so wet that I know it's coating all over his cock, just like I know he's going to let me ride him and then push me down on the bed and fuck me so hard that I still feel him when I'm walking around tomorrow.

I know it... and God, I want it.

"If he fucks up, you can kill him," I tell him, hoping like hell that Chains isn't that stupid.

"You seem awful calm about this, Nicole."

"Because, this way we get grandkids."

"I'm too young for grandkids," he growls, watching my body move back and forth. If he keeps playing with me like this I'm going to come before he ever gets inside of me.

"Just think, Dragon. We can spoil them, and love them and then send them home and run around the house naked and have sex whenever we want."

"You've been thinking about this a lot."

"Oh yeah," I grin down at him.

"Greedy pussy," he mutters, making me grin. "Reach down and bring me home, Mama," he orders, his voice guttural and hoarse, his head tilted back, his eyes closed.

When he's like this, I lose my breath. All these years and I still look at him and see such fucking beauty. Beauty hiding beneath the surface of a man that is bigger than life.

A man who is and has always been my whole world.

I lift up on my knees, wrapping my hand around his cock. It's slick and wet with our combined juices. His cock jerks and throbs in my hand as I line him up with my entrance.

"Dragon," I whine, whimper... hell, I'm begging.

His beautiful eyes open and he looks at me and just like that day at the gas station, my heart flips over in my chest.

"I love you, Mama," he vows as I slide down on him.

"Forever," I moan.

"Forever," he says, kissing me, and swallowing my cries of pleasure as I lose myself in the magic of making love with my husband.

40

CHAINS

"You and I are going for a little ride, Chains."

That's all he said, but that, I guess, was enough. One thing I've learned about Dragon is that he's a man who doesn't waste words. I've healed up mostly from my earlier beatings, and I was definitely right, Dragon had been pulling his punches lately. I'm still sore as hell, and one of my eyes is a fucking mess, but I made it to Dragon's cage—a decked out King Ranch Blue Ford F-250—on my own and I am rather proud of that accomplishment. Kayden's brothers followed close behind, but neither of them spoke either. I guessed they must be a lot like their father, which suited me fine.

Dragon and I have been driving for what feels like days, but what in reality has been hours. I haven't been paying attention where we're going, because honestly, it's the first time I've been out in the sun in practically two weeks and that shit is hell on a head that's already hurting. I could use my shades that I keep on my bike, but at this point I don't even know where Betty is. Dragon's twisted enough that I figure he had it melted down. It's what I would have done in his shoes.

Finally, I can feel the truck coming to a slow stop. I guess I was half asleep because the sound of Dragon's door opening, jars me to full attention. I jerk up slowly, squinting against the sun so that I can see around me and frown. It's a gas station, vaguely familiar, although I guess that doesn't matter. I suppose he needed a fill up. In the side mirror I can see three bikes pull in behind us. It appears Dragon has his posse with us.

The thought occurs to me that he let me heal up just to kill me. I really thought I possessed common sense, even thought I was pretty damn smart. Underestimating a man, especially when you're fucking his daughter is not smart at fucking all.

"Get out," Dragon orders when he jerks my door open.

"I do need to shake the dew off the lily," I mutter, acting as if I have a choice. I practically have to slide out of the truck, but I manage to do it without falling completely to my knees and I'm silently congratulating myself.

"If I was you, motherfucker, I'd refrain from saying anything about your damn dick. I still think I should cut that motherfucker off," Dragon barks, his voice low but you can still hear the anger that is thick in every word.

Definitely underestimated the man.

I start to walk, thinking we're headed to the restroom, when without warning, Dragon kicks my legs out from under me. Now, I'd like to say I'm still healing from my beatdown, but the truth is that again I misread Dragon and wasn't prepared. If I have any hope of coming out of this shit alive, I need to stop that shit and start paying better attention.

"Fuck," I groan as I hit the concrete ground.

When I look up, Dragon, Dancer, and Dragon's two boys are standing around me.

"What the fuck?" I growl, getting tired of this bullshit. If the asshole is going to kill me, he needs to do it, because I'm going to end him first at this rate, and that's probably something Kayden will never forgive me for. And, if I live, you better believe I'm keeping Kayden. Daddy here, will just have to get used to it.

"This place look familiar dick-weed?"

I look around and I can admit that right now my brain is slow to process shit.

"It's a damn gas station," I snap.

"Look again, motherfucker. Maybe you need something to prod your memory? Maybe I should use those chains around your hands to attach your ass to the fucking steering wheel, like you did my daughter. What do you think?"

Shit. Okay, now I know where we're at. We're actually in the same exact spot I was parked at that day. Is this where Dragon means to kill me? Shit, I can even kind of respect that. I wish I could find reasons to hate him for what he's doing but I can't. *Not really.* I've never had kids, but I reckon if I did, I'd be a lot like this asshole. I pull on my chains, trying to figure out how I'm going to get out of this. I might be calm about all this shit, but I don't really want to die. I just gained everything, I sure as hell don't want to give it up without a fight.

"You're not talking," Dragon growls. "That pile of shit you have in your head in place of brains putting anything together yet?"

"Yeah. I know where I am," I admit, my voice raw. "What fucking game are you playing? Let me out of these damn things," I tell him, shaking my hands to make the links clink together. "And let's have this out man to man."

"Only problem with that, is we'd be short one fucking man," Dragon growls and he kicks me in the side with his booted foot.

It definitely hits the mark, slamming into my ribs and hurting so fucking bad that it robs me of breath. I flinch, but I do my best not to curl in to the fucking fetal position like I want to.

"Go fuck yourself," I tell him, my voice weak and sounding pathetic, even to my own ears.

"You left my daughter out here in her car alone, motherfucker. You left her cuffed to damn steering wheel in a tinker-toy car, with the fucking windows down. You left her alone and unprotected, and you want me to believe you care about her?"

"I kept my eye on her, she was fine. I wasn't gone but a damn minute," I growl, pissed off now by what he's insinuating. Kayden is mine. I protect her and I sure as hell will keep a closer eye than he did on her. He left her all alone and didn't even know I was sniffing around her. When Kayden and I have kids, you can sure as hell believe that shit won't happen.

Dragon kicks me again, and this time Dancer does the same, and Dom and Thomas do too, and if I'm not mistaken they kick a lot fucking harder than the first two. I wheeze and cough, yell out —as much as I can—and pull myself up so I'm sitting. I'm not going to just lie here and become their damn punching bag.

Dragon, grabs me by my hair, yanking my head back and I go to fight him, but he pulls out a gun, pushing the end of the barrel hard against my temple. I try to look around, but the place is eerily quiet. There's no one here.

How does that happen?

"You left her alone for seven minutes and forty-nine and a half seconds, motherfucker. It would just take me about three seconds to splatter your brains on this fucking ground. That's it. You left my daughter *alone* for seven minutes and forty-nine and a half seconds. Do you know what could have happened to her in that time?"

So this is how it ends. He's going to shoot me here and there's not much I can do to stop it. I sure as hell refuse to beg him for my life.

"She was fine. I kept an eye on her."

"You kept an eye on her," he repeats. You kept an eye on her," he says again, this time it's almost as if he's laughing at the words, but there's no mistaking the fury on his face.

"Were you keeping an eye on her when she stretched and cried out in pain, all to reach her damn burn phone under the seat to call me and beg for your fucking life, Nomad?"

"I..."

Shit. I wasn't.

I did keep looking at her through the window, but I had to pay for the gas and I took a quick piss, before I came back out to get her to do the same.

"You're not so talkative now, are you, motherfucker? Now, I've decided to give you a quick lesson in life, because evidently, you're too fucking stupid to have caught on sooner. You're in the club life, by dipping your toes in the water, but you don't live the life."

"Bullshit," I snarl.

Dragon ignores me, or at least for the most part he does. He's crouched down now. Still holding me by my hair, but he's letting the head of his gun move back and forth, grazing against my temple.

"As a nomad, you may have loyalty to certain brothers, but you don't really have a home, do you? You haven't pledged yourself to a club, you don't have to worry about territories, you just go where you want and piss in the wind."

I remain quiet. I can hear the contempt he has for my lifestyle and I could give two-shits about it. I've enjoyed how I lived my life. Not until I met Kayden, did I ever think I wanted anything else. Since being with her, I will admit, I've been thinking differently. I want to put down roots and have a home for our kids and I want to do that for me, but also for Kayden, because I know that's the life she wants and I want to be the asshole who gives that to her. I don't want to give another man the chance to give her happiness.

That's my job.

Or rather it was going to be. The feel of Dragon's gun pushing into my temple again, reminds me that it may never happen now.

"Me and my men? We don't have that luxury. We fought, we bled, and some of my men died to secure our territory. We have to *worry* about territories."

"Just fucking shoot me and get this over with," I mutter, thoughts of not spending my life with Kayden make my gut clench. There was more I needed to say to her, more I needed to do…

He slaps the side of the barrel against my head, but the top of it—not the temple. Again, I get the feeling that he's not trying to seriously harm me. It's the same feeling I've been getting for at least a week.

"I'm being nice and giving you a lesson you need to get. Pay fucking attention or I will shoot you, but I won't end you quick. I'll stomp your fucking balls into the ground until you bleed out from them slowly. You feel me?"

"I'm listening," I tell him, because suddenly I am. I think he has something he is telling me now and he's not doing this shit to just torture me and get his rocks off—though he probably is enjoying that part.

Dragon seems satisfied with my answer. I can tell this by the way he pulls back, moving the gun away from me and looks me in the eye.

"This here station? It's not in my territory, motherfucker. It's not in any of my allies territories. There's a chance that the fuck load of money and guns I paid to come here for our history lesson won't be enough and we could get waylaid. But, I felt it important enough to try so I did it. Don't worry. I got men close even if you can't see them, and if we do get ambushed, we'll take cover behind your fucking corpse," he says, but I get it. I'm paying a fucking lot of attention now and I understand Dragon's anger so much more now.

"Fuck," I hiss, realizing what a wet-behind-the-ears, fucking prick that I've been.

"I see it's starting to dawn on you. This here is the Demon Chaser's territory. They hate my club. They want me gone, but they know that would take more money and firepower than they have, so we stay away from each other. Now, thanks to you, they have a little more of both and I'm going to take that out of your hide today. Lucky for you, if you listen, I probably won't kill you, because I still have a hell of a lot more than them. But you see, Nomad, that's how these things go. You stay on top as long as you have the strength to back it up. You can't show weaknesses, because a weakness is like exposing an artery. Your enemies will cut that fucking thing open and laugh as you bleed out and dance in the mess you leave behind. I been in this shit for a long time. Early on, I realized I didn't want weaknesses. I couldn't afford them, and rule and protect my men like I needed to. Then, I saw a blue-eyed blonde, with bare feet and my plans went out the fucking window. Do you get what I'm saying yet?"

"Yeah, I get it. Kayden is a weakness."

"There might be hope for you yet, Nomad. Kayden and Nicole are my biggest weaknesses. The boys, they're strong, they're of the age now that they know the score and they can stand on their own. Girls? Our girls need to be protected. They need to be fucking cherished and never—*fucking never*—left in a damn vehicle, chained, with no hope of escape in the middle of enemy territory. You might go where you want, having no club to answer to, and no worry about territory, but my daughter is Savage Brothers property. She *has* enemies."

"You're right. I wasn't thinking. I'm a fucking moron," I growl, pissed off at myself and knowing nothing I can say will make this up. Shit, chills are running through me at the thought of what could have happened to Kayden. Guilt, disgust and delayed fear are rolling in my stomach. If I had lost Kayden, been the reason that she got hurt or died...

"I can see reality is finally sinking in that weak-ass brain of yours. So, I think we've had enough history lesson for today. Besides, I need to hurry this along. Being in DC's territory this long is leaving a bad taste in my mouth. We'll conclude class today with a couple lessons for the future."

"Lessons?" I ask, confused as fuck, pissed off at myself and just a little hopeful I might get to hold Kayden in my arms again.

"The first lesson is simple. You're going to live by three rules from here out Chains."

"What are those?" I ask, not bothering to argue. He's apparently planning on letting me live and that's good enough for now.

"First rule," he says and I wait. "You protect Kayden with that sorry life of yours. Her wellbeing comes first in every fucking thought you have. You slack on that, and there won't be any more second chances. I'll gut you and I'll enjoy gutting you."

I nod, not saying anything, because he's completely right and I will do that, thought I had been doing that, but definitely will pay more attention to the details from here on out.

"Second rule, I made a vow to my woman that I would make sure that I made her nothing but happy for the rest of her life. That's a vow that I'm going to keep and any man that threatens that will die."

"Uh… Okay," I mutter, never having met his wife, I'm not sure what I have to do with this rule, but Dragon clears that up next.

"And finally, my woman loves her daughter. Anyone that takes Kayden away and makes it so she doesn't get to see her often, would make her very *unhappy*. Are you getting a picture here?"

"Yeah man, I got it."

"You need to take it in, Nomad, because if you don't…"

"I got it. I swear," I growl, I'm feeling like a fucking idiot. I don't need his shit piling it on.

"Good enough, but I'll be watching you."

"Are we done here?"

"Are you going to follow the rules?"

"If I stay in the area, I may need to have ties with a local club. Giving up my lifestyle was already a given, that life's not made for Kayden." I mutter.

Dragon watches me closely, but he doesn't respond either way. I don't say anything else. I figure I don't need to.

"Are we done here?" I finally ask, after neither of us make a move to speak.

"With your first lesson, yeah. Now, you get your second lesson," he says, standing up, taking off my chains, and then, looks at his other men.

I might have been an idiot that could have gotten Kayden killed, but I'm clearly seeing what my next lesson is going to be. I force my weak legs to stand. I refuse to remain on the ground while four men beat the fuck out of me. I turn to look at Kayden's brothers, well two men and two boys. They might be her brothers, but I thought they were fucking my woman before I knew that tidbit, so I don't especially like them right now. I'll enjoy getting my licks in on them. I'm hoping I can get a few in on Dragon before I go down.

"Look at that, you know what's coming. You are getting smarter, Nomad."

"Thanks," I mumble, positioning myself so I have all of them in my eyesight.

"Don't look so worried. You just have to take on me and the boys. Dancer is just here to keep time."

"Time?" I ask.

"Yeah, cause the three of us are going to fuck you up for seven minutes and forty-nine and a half seconds," he grins, and the grin is full-on evil.

"You're a twisted, motherfucker," I growl.

"Not the first time that I've heard that, but I figure you need to know just how long that time can be. Don't worry, I'll take it easy on you for the first couple of minutes."

"Just let me have it old man, I can handle you," I snarl, knowing I'm going to get my ass kicked. Dragon may have years on me, but I've felt his hits. He's got fucking power in those arms of his.

"Oh I'm going to enjoy this," he laughs and as he delivers his first hit, I manage to hit back. He connects with my stomach, on a blow that's so damn hard it threatens to buckle my knees. I uppercut him with a growl, thankful that they seem intent on doing this one man at a time instead of all three of them getting me at once.

"So am I," I yell as slam my fist into his jaw. Dragon spits blood at me, giving an unholy grin and then he hits me so hard I think I fucking see stars.

It's then that I decide I must truly love Kayden, there's no other reason I'd be willing to go through this shit....

41

KAYDEN

"I want my man back and if you don't let him go, I'm prepared to do what I have to do to make it happen."

I sound firm. I sound resolute and I sound pissed as hell —all of which I am. Dad's had Chains hidden from me for like two weeks. If Uncle Dancer hadn't been coming by to tell me that Chains was okay, I'd have been going insane. He asked me to be patient. He told me that Dad was slowly coming to terms and warming up to Chains. I don't know what in the hell that even means, but I'm done waiting.

Dad looks up at me from behind his desk. I figured the first thing he would do is yell at me for coming to the club. He doesn't. Instead, he leans back in his chair and studies me. He looks at me so intently and for so long that I have to fight the urge to shift around, betraying my nerves. I haven't said much to my father—except for yelling at him—since the day he showed up at the cabin. I'm hurt, mad and a million other things and I hate it. My father has always been my hero and I've always been his baby. He spoiled me, and I knew it. I don't know what to do with this new relationship that we have.

"Where did the time go?" Dad mutters, and my brow wrinkles in confusion as I try to understand what he's asking.

"I don't—"

"It seems like yesterday that we brought you home from the hospital. I swear you were the prettiest thing I'd ever seen in my life. You had me wrapped around your finger instantly, just like your mom."

"Dad..."

"I'm sorry, Princess."

There's so much sadness on his face, regret that it makes my heart hurt. I've never seen my father look like that.

"What for?"

"For calling you names. I know it hurt you. I get angry and I say shit without thinking. That's not an excuse, it's just the truth and I'm sorry."

I swallow down the emotion that threatens to choke me, and walk around Dad's desk to stand beside him. I lean against it, letting it hold me up because my legs feel more than a little weak.

"Dad, I need you to let Chains go."

"You really love him?" Dad asks.

I take a deep breath and let the emotion shudder through me. I look straight at my dad because I need him to see the truth.

"With all my heart."

"Why did he kidnap you?"

"You haven't asked him?" I ask, surprised.

"He and I haven't really been talking."

"Dad, please tell me you haven't hurt him," I whisper, scared.

"Nothing he won't recover from."

"Oh God, Dad you have to—"

"He lives in this world, Kayden. He'll be fine. He understands."

"I live in this world and I'm not sure I do."

"It's different. Tell me why he kidnapped you."

"I'm not sure you can call it kidnapping, I kind of wanted to go with him," I tell him, summoning up a weak smile.

"Not at first, Princess. I saw the surveillance tapes. Hell, he chained you to a steering wheel at a gas station."

"Dad—"

"Don't take up for him, Kayden. That was in a rival's territory. What the fuck would have happened if one of the DC's would have gotten their hands on you? Do you even understand what the fuck went through my mind when I saw that tape?"

"I… I didn't realize we were in their territory," I mumble, lamely. I don't have a lot to do with the club life, but I do know that the DC's are constantly giving Dad and the club trouble. I also know what it would mean if they got their hands on me. It doesn't excuse it, but it does explain why my father—who is never really calm when it comes to his kids—has been this bad.

"You need to tell me what happened, Kayden."

Confession time. It's not something I'm looking forward to, and I'd rather not tell him, but I need to make him understand that Chains is a good man.

"Thomas called me and asked me to come to the club and pick him up. There was a party going on, so I waited outside. While I was there, I noticed Chains standing there with Twinkies draped all over him."

"And that's the kind of man you want? A man who goes for easy pussy when he has a good woman? Do you think your mom would put up with that shit?"

"No and that's why I wouldn't go with him willingly. But, I misread it. He says I would have seen him knocking them away, if I had kept watching."

"And you believe him?"

"I completely and utterly, believe him, Dad. Chains would never lie to me."

"He's a damn drifter, Princess. You don't want to live the club life. You had plans. Do you really think Chains can give you the life you want?" Dad asks, bringing up a very good point.

"I honestly don't know what will happen, Dad, but that's something that Chains and I need to figure out. It's time you let me grow up."

"You're too damn young."

"I'm not that much younger than Mom was when she met you, Daddy."

"That seems like a lifetime ago. Damn, she was something else back then. Still is, but back then she was hell on wheels. She busted a Twinkie's nose once over similar shit. She could probably give you pointers on that shit, Princess."

"I know, she told me. Will you let Chains go, Daddy?"

"If he hurts you, I'll kill him."

"Is that a yes?"

"He's already free. Doc is checking him out in Gun's old room. You can go to him there."

"I don't have to have an escort to go to the rooms?" I ask surprised, because the few times I have, Dad or my uncles have been with me.

"If you're going to be an Old Lady, you're going to see more shit than I can shield you from," he says, not sounding happy about it.

"Thank you, Daddy!" I cry, moving into my father to hug him.

His arms go around me tight, holding me against his solid body. For a minute, I'm transported back in time. Back when I truly was Daddy's little girl and he would hold me when I cried.

"You're my heart, Kayden. You and your brothers are the best of your mother and me, but you've always been my special miracle. This Chains better always take care of you. I see him doing one thing to hurt you and I'll end him, Princess. Your tears won't be enough to save him."

"I love you, Daddy," I whisper into his shoulder, feeling tears prick at the back of my eyes.

"I love you, Princess, with my entire soul."

I squeeze him tight and he kisses my forehead. I turn to walk away, I have the door opened and am about to leave when Dad stops me.

"And Princess?"

"Yeah, Dad?"

"I told him and I'll tell you. It would break your mother's heart if he took you away from us. Anything that breaks your mother's heart and makes her sad, I'll destroy. That includes his sorry ass."

"Love you, Daddy," I repeat.

"Love you, too," he says, his voice sounding pensive and I know it's hard for Dad to accept that I'm not his baby any longer.

I shake it off, because I need to get to Chains. I just pray that he still wants to see me after everything my father has put him through.

42

CHAINS

"Fuck," I hiss, sitting up on the bed.

I'm better, but still sore as hell. It's been two days since my beat down at the gas station. I held my own for a bit with Dragon, although I have to admit he got the better of me. I'd like to say it's because I was still healing from the earlier fights, but the truth is I'm not sure I could take Dragon down even if I was completely healthy. It's something I'd like to try one day. I got some good hits in on Dom and Thomas, but I have to admit they aren't slouches with their fists either. Still, I took them for the most part, and at least I feel better about that. The three of them had to help me back in the truck and I have to admit Dragon was right about something. I will *never* forget how long seven minutes and forty-nine and a half seconds is ever again. Although, to be fair, after thinking of leaving Kayden during that time, in enemy territory, I would have never forgotten that ever again. I was completely stupid. My only excuse is that I never had to worry about whose territory I was in, and it just didn't occur to me. I won't make that mistake anymore.

I'm in the damn club house now after being stitched up by the club doctor and yet another stern warning from Dragon that I better never hurt Kayden or make his wife cry. He told me that his daughter would be by to see me sometime today and then he stomped out. He put the emphasis on the words *his daughter*, but it was said in what I'm learning is 'Dragon-talk'. I think that letting her come by to see me means that Kayden is truly mine now. At least I think so. Hell, I'm not allowed to leave this room, so who knows what he has planned next. I can hear a man outside the door, so I know I'm still under guard.

"Chains."

My head jerks to the open door and Kayden is standing there. Fuck, it's been weeks since I've seen her, but she's so much better than even my memory of her could recall. Her hair is down. Her curls are piling over and over in waves, all the way down to her shoulders. She's wearing a white slouchy sweater, that still manages to curve around her breasts, and jeans that hug her ass like a second skin. She's the prettiest thing I've ever seen in my life.

"Get over here, Baby Girl," I demand. My voice is hoarse and full of emotion. Fuck, it almost feels like I can't breathe. I know I've been aching for her, missing her so much that the ache was constant, but Jesus, now that I've seen her again, I realize the pain of being away from her was even more than I guessed.

She closes the door, and when she turns back to me she seems nervous and unsure. She takes another step and then another and as she gets closer I can see the tears shining in her eyes.

"What has he done to you?" she whispers, the words thick on her tongue and heavy with sadness.

"I'm fine. Get your ass over here and hug your man."

"Oh, Baby," she whispers, dropping down to her knees in front of me and holding me close. Pain sears through me as she hugs, but I don't give a fuck. It just feels damn good that she's in my arms again. I breathe her scent into my lungs and hold her close. She pulls back to look at me, her hand lain tenderly along my jawline. "Your poor beautiful face," she weeps.

A startled laugh leaves me and that hurts like hell, because I wasn't expecting it and my face is sore as fuck.

"Baby, not sure my face has ever been pretty."

"Everything about you is pretty."

I push my fingers in her hair, holding her neck to pull her back and make her look at me. I need those eyes on me. I need to touch her, believe that this is real, and that I'm not imagining this shit. "Baby."

"I'm going to kill my Dad."

"You're going to leave him alone."

"Bullshit, have you seen what he did to you?"

"Didn't need to see it, Baby. I was there, but yeah, I caught a glimpse in the mirror after my shower this morning. It's not as bad as I expected."

"Not as bad... Oh my God!"

"Cool it, Kayden. I'm good and more importantly, I have you."

"Have... You still want me? After all of the shit you've been through?"

"Fuck, woman. After all of the shit I've been through, if I don't get you out of it, I'll kill these assholes."

"That's some mighty big words, coming from a punk who had to be lifted into my truck a couple days ago," Dragon laughs from the door.

"Dad! I can't believe what you've done. How could you do this to Chains?" she cries, jerking against my hold and even though it hurts like hell, I hold her back, refusing to let her go.

"Kayden, stop," I tell her, my voice firm, though trying to soften it just enough not to piss her off.

"Stop?" she asks and from the look on her face, I'm thinking my whole trying to go easy thing, didn't work. There's sparks flying in those dark chocolate eyes and they're shooting fire at me.

"Your father had every right to hand me my ass. I didn't watch after you like I should have and I fucked up."

"Have you seen your face, because I have and I hate to imagine what I'm going to find when you take your clothes off," she huffs.

"That won't happen until he puts a ring on it," Dragon says, his voice deadly.

"Excuse me?" Kayden screeches and if my head wasn't pounding and I didn't want some alone time with my woman, to reassure myself that she was really here, I'd enjoy watching them go after one another.

"This is between me and the Nomad," Dragon says, crossing his arms at his chest.

"You're talking about my life and in particular my *sex* life with my boyfriend, Dad. It involves me."

"You want your man to stay alive, Kayden, you're going to let me live in the dream world where you're still a virgin, untouched and wanting to watch Toy Story," Dragon growls.

"I… Dad you gave me your blessing on my relationship with Chains. What do you think we are going to do? We're both adults."

"Not in my eyes," Dragon shrugs, his eyes never leaving my face, so I'm doing my best to hide my smile—but, it's not easy.

"Are you being for real right now?" Kayden huffs. "What in the hell do you think we're going to do together in bed?"

"Until I see you married, nothing. After that, I don't need a play by play. In my eyes you'll be drinking that grape Kool-aid shit you like and playing that damn game you used to drive me fucking bonkers with."

"What game?"

"That fucking game where you kept trying to pick fruit off the trees and then you'd cry because you always landed on that damn dog."

"I... Cherry O? Really? You're going to imagine that Chains and I are playing Hi Ho Cherry O in bed?"

"On your wedding night. You won't be in his bed before then. That's final."

"You cannot give me ultimatums about when I have sex with my boyfriend. I can't believe you. Isn't it enough that you've held him hostage for weeks and almost killed him?"

"Please, he barely got a slap on the wrist. I think I'm being very hospitable."

"Hospitable? Now you're just shitting me. You don't even know that word. If you do, then you think it means not cutting off a body part on someone."

"Your point? The Nomad still has all his body parts, though I got to tell you girl, it was a close thing and if you keep giving me lip, that could change."

"You put your hands back on Chains and I'll make you sorry, Daddy. I love you, but I'm not putting up with this shit anymore. Chains is my man and if I want to have sex with him every day and twice on Sunday from this day forward then I will. What we do together only concerns two people and one of those isn't you."

"Nomad?"

"Yeah, Dragon."

"You gonna lock her down?"

Fuck. Everything is a fucking test with this asshole.

"Kayden, leave me and your Dad alone for a few minutes."

"You have got to be shitting me."

"Baby Girl, just do it."

"The fuck I will! I'm not letting him push us into marriage. That's just crazy. We will have sex anytime we feel like it and there isn't a damn thing he can do about it."

"Kayden, woman, I love you, but if you keep it up you're going to get me killed. Let me and your Dad talk and say what needs to be said."

"I... You love me?"

"Jesus, do you think a man would take a beating like I have and then, survive a showdown with your brothers just for fun? I want this, if I didn't, I wouldn't still be hanging around."

She rubs her lips together, her arms crossed at her chest and I can see her father is holding his hands in much the same way. That spells trouble for me in the future, because fuck if I don't think she's just as stubborn as her father. I shake my head, because even that's not enough to make me walk away. I'm never walking away from Kayden.

"We're not done talking about this," she says, her voice soft, her eyes even softer and she's staring at me as if I've somehow hung the moon. A man would gladly die for a look like that.

"I didn't think we were, Baby."

"I love you, Chains."

"I know, Kayden."

"The correct response is, I love you, too, asshole," she mutters, turning away from me and walking to the door where her dad is standing. He moves aside for her to leave. She stops at the threshold and looks up at her dad.

"I love you, too, but you're an asshole, Dad."

"Your mother likes to tell me that often."

"She's a wise woman," Kayden mutters, leaning up on her tiptoes to kiss her dad on the cheek. If I didn't know I was in love before, I do now, because watching her kiss her own father pisses me off. Those lips belong to me now.

"I know, she married me," Dragon quips, and the grin on his face gives him the look of a very satisfied man.

"Kayden," I growl cause she kisses him again.

Damn it, this being owned by a woman is going to take some getting used to. I never saw myself as the pussy-whipped type, but I definitely am in this case. Dragon takes one look at my face and busts out laughing. The bastard knows I'm in deep shit and he's enjoying it. Kayden ignores me, instead she tries to sign my death warrant.

"Oh, and Dad? That game you were talking about? It was the bird I kept landing on and not just fruit, but cherries. And just so you know, we played that game I landed on the bird and the cherry—"

"Fucking hell, Kayden. Are you trying to get me killed?" I bark.

And what does my woman do?

She laughs.

"Fine, fine I'm going. Jesus, men are such assholes. I don't even know why I bother," she adds, walking out.

"Because you love me," I growl, not liking her comment at fucking all.

"Yeah, I do," she says, surprising me. I stare at her, watching her lips spread into a smile and I'm lost all over again. I'm not sure how long we stay like that, but Dragon clears his throat and breaks the trance. She blows me a kiss and leaves, leaving me with her dad.

Neither of us speak for a while. I don't know why he doesn't. I don't because I know what's coming, so I just wait.

"You're going to marry her."

"Definitely."

"You'll not be having sex with my daughter. She's not a whore, she's a good woman. You lock it down with a ring on her finger first."

"You've lived the club life. You want me to believe you had your ring on your old lady's hand before you fucked her?"

"Hell no. But I'm me. You are just you and this is *my* daughter."

I shake my head in disbelief, but I do it smiling, because he's an asshole, but I have to admit he's kind of growing on me—like a damn fungus.

"The wedding is going to have to be damn quick. We're talking, tomorrow."

"Two weeks."

"Two weeks? No fucking way."

"I need to see you can stick to your word."

"Kayden's right. You are a fucking asshole."

"Yeah I know. While we're on the subject, we both know the club life. There's not a damn thing wrong with it. Twinkies have their place in this world, but if I ever see you with another woman, or catch a breath of it, I'll snap your neck. I won't have you hurting my daughter."

"Christ man. Kayden is a fucking handful. Do you really see me having the energy for more?"

"She is a chip off the old shoulder," he brags.

"I'm trying to ignore that fact. If I didn't, I'd be running for the hills."

"Fuck you," he laughs. "So, we have an agreement?"

"Do I have a choice?"

"Not a fucking one," Dragon says, grinning.

"I didn't think so. But, just so you know, I can vow to you that there will never be another woman for me except Kayden. You don't have no worries when it comes to the club girls or anyone else."

"Good to know," Dragon says. "This door stays open while Kayden is in here," he adds, turning to walk out.

The bastard.

"Besides, your girl wears a man out. There's no way I could summon up the strength to look at another woman once she's done with me," I yell out.

"I should have fucking killed you when I had the chance. You should thank my wife when you see her, Chains. If not for her, you'd be two feet under."

"Two feet? Don't you mean six?"

"Nah, you need to be close to the surface for the vultures to eat off of your hide," he calls back and then he's gone, leaving me shaking my head, wondering just how crazy life will become with Dragon as a father-in-law.

43

KAYDEN

"I can't believe you right now. No, Chains. Absolutely not."

He mutters under his breath and then releases a breath that makes it clear he's unhappy. He actually looks and sounds like a grizzly bear when they hit their favorite picnic spot, only to find out there are no left overs or people to maul.

"Kayden, you said you loved me."

"And I do, although, I'm getting seriously worried about your sanity at this point."

"Jesus, woman. I'm just asking you to marry me, not go on a Bonnie and Clyde killing spree across country."

"You're not *asking* me to marry you. You're *telling* me to marry you and there's a big difference," I respond and I do it while wondering if I can kick him in the balls and not truly hurt him. He's still recovering from Dad's stupidity—not to mention my brothers, too. I don't want to do more damage, but obviously Chains needs something to make his brain start functioning again.

"Fine, Kayden Nicole West, will you marry me?"

He's sitting up on the bed with his boxers on—and just to be clear, my man doesn't wear boxers normally. He's strictly commando all the way.

"So freaking romantic," I mutter, getting more and more pissed off by the second.

"Woman, why are you busting my balls? You said you love me."

"Oh my God, you're even starting to sound like him," I cry, my hands tightening up in fists, because I literally have to resist the urge to slap some sense into him.

"What are you talking about now?"

"You're starting to sound like my father! Stop it! Stop it right now!"

"Kayden, quit being a bitch. I'm not in shape to spank your ass right now. I'm not in the shape to argue with you either. We're getting married and that's final."

"We are *not* getting married. I don't want to get married. I have school to finish and—"

"Baby Girl, I'm not going to keep you from going to school."

"Chains, you live life on the road. There's no going to school when I'm on the back of a bike most of the time."

"We'll settle down. Stay in one spot, keep you close to your family."

"Now, I know you're insane. This is not you talking. I don't know who it is, but it's not you. You're giving me all the answers my father would approve of. That's not what I want."

"Jesus. Fucking hell, Kayden. Tell me what you want, because I'm tired of trying to figure it out. I thought women wanted weddings—especially when they're supposed to love their man. What? Was I just a way to tell your father to go fuck himself and now that he's on board, you're just going to tell me fuck off?"

"I... You... Oh my God! You did *not* just say that."

"I think it's pretty damn clear, I did."

"You know what, Chains? If you think that's who I am? Then *you* can go *fuck* yourself!" I growl and then, I turn and stomp out.

I make it all the way to the door when Chains wraps his arm around me and secures me against his body.

"Oh no you don't," he growls. He pulls me back and slams the door shut. My body goes tight and I fight against his hold. "You and I are going to have this shit out, Kayden. I told you when you gave yourself to me that there was no going back and damn it, there's not. You're mine and there will be no walking away from me—*from us.*"

"Shouldn't you open the door back? Aren't you afraid your new best friend will be pissed you're going against his rules?"

"Is that what has your panties in a wad, Baby Girl? That I haven't killed your father? Did you want me to kill the motherfucker?" he growls.

I kick against him and he lets me go. I know that's proof he's still in bad shape, which just makes me madder.

"Don't be disgusting!"

"Then, what in the fuck is your problem, Kayden? Jesus, I'm too fucking old for these games. Just tell me what in the hell is going on in your head."

"You're changing and I don't like it."

"Change is a fact of life, Kayden. It just happens. Maybe if you could tell me what in the hell I've done you dislike so fucking much..."

"You're agreeing to everything my dad is saying! I mean, look at you. You're wearing damn underwear, for Christ's sake!"

"I'm wearing underwear because I'm in a clubhouse with a bunch of men and Twinkies. You'd rather I be lying in bed naked? Will that make you calm your ass down? Fine," he growls, grabbing the waist band of his boxers and pushing them down, quickly—quicker than I thought he could have with his injuries —kicking them to the side and leaving him completely naked. His cock is semi-aroused, and bobbing out and damn it, I forgot how big he is, and how wide, and how beautiful, and how mouth-watering and... "My face is up here, Baby Girl," he grumbles, still definitely annoyed and snapping me out of momentary thought derailment.

"Oh my God! Put some clothes on Chains!"

"Kayden, you just told me to take them off. I swear if you didn't make me want to kiss you so much, I'd strangle you," he grunts, not bothering to get dressed.

He flops back down on the bed and that's when I notice a fine bead of sweat along his forehead. Guilt hits me, because he's not doing as well as he would have me believe. It's been two days since I finally got him back and I've been spending most of my time here at the club—although not the night time. My nights have been texting with Chains, but it all feels empty. I miss him when he is not around and this whole marriage thing is seriously stressing me out.

I walk over to the bed and grab the sheet and pull it up over his body. I talk a big game, but I don't want to get Chains killed either. I'm also not real fired up to have my father walk in on me and Chains again either. That's an experience that no one needs to relive, ever.

"I'm sorry," I mutter, lying down on the bed beside him. "You're not up to fighting and here I am driving you crazy."

"You're being a bitch, but fuck, I even kind of like that," Chains grumbles pulling me closer, one hand going to cup my ass, as he kisses the top of my head.

"You're so sweet," I mumble against his chest, breathing him in and letting his heartbeat play in my ear, soothing me.

"Tell me what's really got you pissed off, Baby Girl."

"Dad's forcing you to marry me. I don't want that for you, Chains. Hell, I don't want it for me. If I get married, I want it to be because the man I love loves me and wants to stand in front of a preacher and declare that love and pledge the rest of our lives together. Not because if he doesn't, my dad will shoot his dick off."

Chains turns on his side, moving my body with him, so I'm

forced to do the same and look at him. He keeps his hand under my chin, his eyes pinning mine with his heated gaze.

"If you don't get that I love you, Kayden, I'm not sure how to make it any clearer. Hell, do you think your father would have let me live, if he couldn't tell how special you are to me?"

"Still, you don't want ties and forever, Chains. Heck, that's how you got your road name. I don't want to force you into something you don't want. Not this—*especially* not this."

"Kayden, I thought you knew me. It felt like you knew me better than anyone ever has before. Do you really think I'd do anything that I didn't want to do?"

"Well, I mean, I don't know. I didn't think so, but here you are agreeing to everything and maybe... I don't know, Chains. I'm just..."

"You're what?"

"I'm scared," I whisper guiltily. "There, I said it. I don't want to marry you and then have you realize that being with me, living our lives together isn't what you wanted. I don't want to be pushed into marriage by my father. I don't want—"

I stop talking when Chains kisses me. I let him, because I'm tired of the chaos in my mind and to be honest, what small kisses we've shared haven't been passionate and maybe that's where part of my worry is coming from. I lose myself in this kiss. It's definitely passionate and Chains is holding me close, the taste of him hits me like heated electricity, sex... hot, sweaty sex, and I want more.

"If I didn't want to marry you, Baby Girl, I'd have already been out of town. I sure as fuck wouldn't have played your father's game this long. I love you. I want our lives together. I want my ring on your finger, my cut on your back, and you on my bike. I don't know how to make that any clearer."

"But you said—"

"I said a lot of bullshit, but how is a man supposed to know what he wants or what's in store for him when he's only half lived? Until I met you and got a taste of you, Kayden, I had no idea."

I close my eyes as the sweetness of his words poor over me.

"There's my man," I whisper, knowing this is what I've missed. This feeling that there's only the two of us at the center of this. That no one else matters, because it's just me and Chains against the world.

"It's good you know that. Are you done arguing with me now, Kayden? 'Cause I swear to you, Baby Girl, you're not getting away from me, even if I have to kidnap you again to make it happen."

"Well, that does sound kind of interesting...." I mumble, my fingers moving against the fine hairs on his chest.

"Christ," he curses, but I can hear the humor in his voice and it makes me smile.

"What if you regret marrying me?" I ask, revealing my biggest worry. Chains has lived on the road for a long time. He's never had true ties, unless you count his sisters. It's not a big stretch to think he might regret his choices. Heck, I don't know anything about being a wife.

"What if you regret marrying me, Kayden?" he asks, surprising me with his question.

"I don't think that's possible, Chains. I love you."

"There's your answer."

"But, I'd be choosing to marry you of my own free will. You don't exactly have that luxury," I remind him, tilting my head back to look at him.

"How about you let me worry about that shit? You trust me enough to take a chance and let me prove to you that marrying you and having you in my life every single day, is exactly what I want."

"I'm not waiting two weeks before we have sex, Chains. I refuse."

"Baby Girl, I made a deal with your father. I gave my word. Two weeks won't be that long."

"Bullshit. We're not waiting," I grumble.

"We are," he says stubbornly.

"How about you keep thinking that, but trust me enough to know that I'm going to make it impossible for you to make it two weeks?"

"Whatever you say," he mutters, but I can see the worry that moves over his face and it makes me grin. I can make Chains break, I just need to get...*creative.*

44

DRAGON

"What are you grinning at, Mama?"

"I was just thinking that I married the most stubborn man on the face of the earth," Nicole says while walking into our room.

"And what brought you to that realization, especially after all of these years?" I ask, not bothering to argue, because I figure she's probably right. Still, I'm a man who has everything he has always wanted but thought he could never have. If that's what being stubborn gets you, then thank God I am.

I turn into her. Nicole wraps her arms around me as I pull her close.

"It's not a new realization, it's just one that needs to be repeated quite often, because it's so true," she jokes.

"The boys and I missed you at dinner."

"Trust me, I would've rather been home, especially on family night. Hell, I would have rather had my teeth all pulled out instead of shopping with Kayden."

Ever since Nicole and I had the kids, we've done our best to make every Wednesday night about our family. We have dinner as a family, we catch up, and reconnect. When Nicole first mentioned it, I thought she was crazy, but as the years passed and the kids got older, I began to love those nights. Sometimes the club shit gets in the way, but I always try like hell to prevent that. I found out early on that Wednesday's with our kids made my woman smile and I wanted to do everything in the world to keep that smile on her face. Nothing is more beautiful than my woman happy and smiling.

"I don't think you need to talk that drastic. I happen to like your teeth, especially when they're biting into me. I thought shopping for dresses was supposed to be fun for girls?"

"Normally, it is, especially for wedding dresses. But I swear, your daughter is so grumpy right now, that the devil couldn't stand her."

I try to hide my grin, I'm pretty sure I fail.

"Sorry you had a rough night, Mama," I tell her, kissing her forehead.

"Did you invite Chains over for family night?"

"YEAH, I invited the bastard over. I'm still not sure why you had me do it, but I did."

"Because he's family now. Besides, if he has to put up with Kayden when she gets in these moods, he going to need us for moral support. How did things go, anyway?"

"He was so grumpy, the devil couldn't stand him," I laugh, feeling pretty satisfied with myself.

"Kayden is mad as hell because Chains won't even touch her. She says it's like she's suddenly became contagious with the Bubonic Plague. Said she's tried everything and I won't go into specifics, but let's just say your daughter has a very big imagination," Nicole mutters. "I've learned things about my daughter that I never wanted to know."

"Yeah, do us both a favor and keep that shit to yourself," I mumble and to stop from even letting my mind go into that direction, I think about how damn miserable Chains was. He was so damn grumpy when Dom and Thomas were giving him shit about blue balls and calling him Father Chains. When they began asking him if it was true that you begin to hallucinate when you're celibate, I have to admit I almost felt sorry for the fucker.

I go to the shower, turning the water valve on and adjusting the water to warm, almost hot.

"Did you truly make Chains promise not to have sex with our daughter until they were married?" Nicole asks, laughing.

"You're damn right I did," I respond. I turn to look at my wife, silently daring her to argue with me on this. Nicole surprises me.

"My man is so smart," she says, unable to hold back her laughter."

"It's about time you realize that," I respond with a wink. Then, I walk to her and begin unbuttoning her shirt.

"What are you doing, Dragon?"

"Undressing my woman, so she can take a shower with me. And, if she's really good, I'm going to let her get on her knees and suck my cock."

"Wow, you're all heart, aren't you?"

"All heart and a big dick," I respond, pulling her shirt from her body and groaning under my breath when her full tits are finally in view, overfilling her red silk bra. Jesus, my woman has the best fucking tits the Man upstairs ever blessed a woman with.

Nicole reaches down and wraps her hand around my cock, stoking him tightly in her hand.

"I told Kayden I'd make you tell Chains that he didn't have to wait."

"Are you going to?" I ask her, barely paying attention because I'm more concerned with taking Nicole's pants off.

"Yeah," she says and I let out a frustrated breath.

"Damn it, Nicole—"

"And when I do," Nicole says, pressing a finger against my

lips, to stop me from talking. "You're going to say no," she adds, shocking me.

"The fuck you say," I laugh out, startled, because I really thought she was going to give me shit. "You're not going to threaten to lock me out of your pussy if I don't?"

"Why would I do that and make myself miserable? Newsflash, Dragon, I like it when you're in my pussy," she grins.

"That definitely makes two of us, Mama."

"Besides your daughter was so bitchy this afternoon, it serves her right."

I throw my head back and laugh, and then I quickly undo Nicole's bra. Next, I push her panties down and she helps me by shimmying out of them really quick. I pick her up in my arms and carry her toward the shower.

"I love your laughter, Dragon." She sighs against my chest as she kisses me there.

"You should, Mama, since you're the one that gave it to me. I didn't have a damn thing in the world to laugh or be happy about until you waltzed in it and brought me light."

"You did the same for me, my love. You've given me everything," she says, emotion so thick in her words that my heart squeezes painfully in reaction.

"I'm about to give you something else, Mama," I mumble. "I've decided since you're being such a good little girl, I'm going to be the one to get on my knees in the shower."

"You are?"

"Yeah, I'm going to eat my woman's greedy little cunt and let her ride my face."

"Fuck yeah," she whispers, the words little more than a breath, as I step into the shower. I hold her gaze as I slip slowly down on my knees, pressing kisses down her body on the slow path to heaven. Then, I make sure to make Nicole scream out in pleasure so loudly that Chains—the poor bastard, can probably hear her. In fact, I'm almost sure of it, considering he got too drunk tonight and is crashing in Kayden's old bedroom.

And if me being happier tonight than I've ever been in my life, because I'm lying in bed with my dick limp from coming over and over in Nicole's hot little body, my woman softly snoring because I've exhausted her, and enjoying all this while picturing Chains and his blue balls trying to sleep in Kayden's twin size bed, with a pink canopy and surrounded by a million stuffed animals, makes me a bastard?

Then I don't give a damn.

I kiss Nicole's temple and fall asleep with a smile.

45

CHAINS

"You okay?"

"Hard not to be fine with three of Dad's men sitting in the back of the room like huge thunderclouds. It kind of puts a damper on the whole bachelorette party," Kayden huffs and I smile, figuring that's safe because she can't see me.

"Just keeping you safe, Baby Girl."

"Whatever. Hope they have fun at the strip club."

"The *what*?" I roar, and I know that the room around me goes quiet, but I ignore them. "What in the hell are you doing at a strip bar?"

"Did he say a strip bar?" I hear Dancer mutter.

"Oh, fuck no. No fucking way," Dragon responds.

"I thought Nailer and Freak were going to keep them under control?" Dom growls, but I ignore them.

"Yes, a strip club. Now if you'll excuse me, I need to go cash in my money and get some dollar bills."

"The fuck you do. That better be a woman stripping on that stage, Kayden, or so help me I'll spank your ass so fucking hard you won't be able to sit."

"Well surprises do happen, Chains, but I'm pretty sure from

the bulge in that banana hammock he's wearing, he's all man. Now, I gotta go, Stud. I'll see you at the wedding tomorrow."

"The fuck you will. You will get out of that damn club right now. The only man's dick you will ever be seeing is mine, woman."

"Jesus, I never knew I could like a man and want to cut off his dick at the same time," Dragon mutters and if I wasn't so pissed off at Kayden right now, I'd flip him off.

"You liked me, Mi Hermano," some dude I don't know replies.

"It was your hand I wanted to cut off if I remember correctly and it was on Nicole's ass at the time. You're lucky you're breathing," Dragon growls.

"Oh no way! You macked on Nicole? Damn, does Mom know?" Diego laughs.

"It was a dark time," the man answers.

I close my eyes, trying to rein in my temper, but it doesn't help.

"Will you motherfuckers cool it so I can hear Kayden?" I yell, figuring that probably signs my death warrant, but I don't much give a fuck right now.

"I'm never getting this strung up over a woman, ever," Hawk mumbles and I shake my head, walking away from the table so I can hear Kayden better.

"Kayden, I'm coming over to get you," I growl. "I'll be there in ten minutes."

"No you won't! I'll remind you that *I* didn't want a marriage, but I'm getting one. You're not seeing me before the wedding because it's bad luck. I'm going to enjoy my bachelorette party, because it seems to be the only fun I'm going to have this week—thanks to you. It's bad enough that I'm having my party the night before my wedding, thanks to Kee-Kee screwing up the dates. But, it's done and it's happening, Chains. So you keep your cute, little ass right where it's at."

"I'm coming to get you, because my woman is *not* looking at another man's dick."

"I don't think they actually bare the dick, unless Jazz and Kee-Kee paid extra for that. They could have, they're both freaks," she mumbles. "Anyway, I gotta go."

"You're not looking at some man's cock. I told you when I took you woman, that mine was the only cock you'd be seeing for the rest of our lives."

"Well, *Stud*, I haven't actually seen your cock in a while have I? So if I get the chance to look at another and remind myself why I want to marry you in the first place, then I will. *Now*, I really gotta go."

"You better not—"

"See ya at the altar, Loverboy," she sing-songs, then hangs up, leaving me to stare at my damn cell in my hand like a fucking moron.

"What?" Gunner asks. He knows me better than anyone and I'm sure he can see the anger I'm trying to hold in.

"I thought your men were watching them? You want to tell me why they're at a fucking strip bar with some man up on stage about to give my woman a lap dance?"

"All the women?" Dom asks, but I ignore him, and keep my gaze leveled on Dragon.

"I'm going to kill Nailer and Freak," Dragon growls.

"You'll have to get in line," I roar, stomping towards the door.

"I'm going with you," Dragon says, falling in step behind me.

"Si, me too. Mi Cielo has some explaining to do."

I hear all the men walking with me, but I don't give a fuck. I just need to get to Kayden.

"This is all your fault," I mumble, to Dragon.

"How in the hell do you figure that?" he snarls as we reach our bikes.

"Because if not for you, I would have fucked Kayden so damn hard that she couldn't have moved, let alone go to this damn party tonight," I tell him, straddling Betty and leaning to push the stand up.

"You're just bound and determined to give me a reason to kill you, Motherfucker," Dragon declares with a scowl, bringing his bike to life with a roar.

I do the same and I squeal out in the lead.

I'm off to claim my woman and remind her I have the only dick she ever needs.

46

KAYDEN

"You did not just do that," Keanna, yells.

"Do what?" I ask, trying to sound innocent, but pretty sure I fail. Mostly, because I'm not. I'm pissed off at Chains. If telling him about Keanna's stripper party gets me laid, then I'm down. If Chains thinks it's cool to withhold dick from me, the bastard better think again. I am not going into a marriage with a man who thinks it's cool not to see to his woman.

"Don't you do what to me, Kay-Kay. You told Chains what we were doing and you did that shit on purpose."

"They'll be here soon," Mom laughs.

"Oh yeah, they will. It's like my party all over again," Aunt Carrie laughs.

"How long do you think we have before they get here?" Aunt Katie asks.

"It's a toss-up to who will be more upset, but I know my man. He will be here in about ten minutes at the most," Aunt Beth responds, looking really calm as she takes a drink of her wine.

"Carrie, you and Skye better get ready to pay me that fifty you owe me," Mom laughs.

"Bitch, I can't believe you," Keanna mutters.

"Hold up! What did you bet money on?" Aunt Katie asks Mom. I have to admit, I'm interested myself.

"Yeah, Mom, why do Aunt Carrie and Skye owe you money?" I ask, looking at the three women in question.

"I said you would get Chains to cave before the wedding. They said there was no way he'd go against Dragon. Obviously, I win," she says with a shrug.

"You seriously bet on whether I'd have sex with Chains before my wedding night?"

"We bet on all kinds of things, don't feel bad," Skye says, patting my shoulder. "Hell, last week we bet on if Nailer's test was going to come back positive for the Clap."

"You did not!" Katie cackles.

"Dude, trust me," Skye says, "With these men it happens. They hate wearing rubbers," she mutters and you can tell she's *really* not happy about that fact. It must be because she's a doctor or something—or maybe because Bull keeps knocking her up.

"Amen to that," Katie says. "I say let the guys show up. That poor man up on stage sure don't have much to be dancing about. My Hunter could put him to shame," she mutters.

"Um.... I don't want to see Uncle Torch stripping on the stage," I tell her, because I really don't. That might put an end to me ever wanting sex again.

"I wouldn't mind seeing some of that action. That man is fine," Keanna says.

"Oh yeah, me too, I always did like older men," Jazz adds.

"Jesus, if I knew how much trouble having a child was, I would have cut off Jacob's dick," Carrie mutters.

"Ew, gross Mom. You aren't supposed to talk about Dad having one of those in front of me. It will make me never want to have sex," Jazz complains.

"Last week, while you were staying with Gabby? We did it in your bed," Carrie says.

"Oh my God!" Jazz screeches.

"That's exactly what I screamed when your father dropped down on his knees and got to work, Dear," Carrie says, so sweetly and calm that you'd think she was discussing the weather.

"I hate you," Jazz yells over all of the laughter, as she stomps out.

"I can't believe you told her that," Katie laughs.

"That girl is going to be the death of Jacob and me. Hawk is my good child. He never gives me grief. But, Jazz? Good Lord, that girl makes me want to choke her most of the time," Carrie sighs.

"Will she come back?" Gabby asks, looking in the direction that Jazz just left.

"She has to. She rode over here with me because her license has been revoked," Carrie responds with a sigh.

"Why was her license revoked?"

"She had fifty-six unpaid tickets."

"Holy fuck! How does that even happen?" Keanna cries.

"She was upset at the officer who wrote her a parking ticket. So, she proceeded to park there every day for two months just to piss him off," Carrie sighs. "She didn't pay them, instead she threw them away. They arrested her and Jacob refused to bail her out. The judge sentenced her to community service and revoked her license for a year."

"Damn," Mom whispers. "You didn't say a word."

"There wasn't much to say. It broke Jacob's heart to let his daughter spent the night in jail. You know how that had to hurt him Nic. You know more than most anyone."

"Yeah," she whispers, her voice going way too soft. The last time I heard Mom use that tone was when our puppy Coda died and she had to break it to Thomas.

He loved that dog.

"This party suddenly got too damn quiet," Keanna mutters. "Time for sausage stuffing time!"

"What?" I ask, only slightly alarmed. After all, I've been friends with Keanna for a long time.

"We got maybe five minutes before your man gets here! I figure that's enough time to see how big of a sausage you can put in your mouth. Everyone line up and those who know their men won't stop them from joining in, get in the back. That way maybe some of the others can play before their guys go all fucking cave man and ruin our fun," Keanna orders.

"I'm behind Kayden, because there's no way Dragon's going to let me play if he gets here first," Mom says.

"Ew, Mom, I don't want to see you stuffing a sausage in your mouth," I complain.

"Then, don't look, Honey," she says, smiling softly, making me roll my eyes.

"Well, I'm playing. Hunter won't care. Hell, he'll pull up a chair and watch. Maybe even offer his own sausage in the mix," Aunt Katie laughs. "He loves public sex."

"Oh gross," Gabby mumbles. "I did *not* need to know that."

"If you didn't know it, you haven't been paying attention to his damn shirts," Aunt Beth laughs from behind Mom. "He did pick out the tank Katie's wearing now, you know."

I probably shouldn't, but for some reason, I can't stop myself and I look at Aunt Katie's hot pink t-shirt.

"My Pink Taco is my man's favorite meal.

For dessert, I give it to him again, in public."

My Uncle Torch is a kinky bastard, but then I've always known that.

"Okay, Kay-Kay! Open wide!" Keanna laughs, grabbing my attention away from Katie's shirt—thank God.

When I look at her, she's holding a giant kielbasa, but it's...

"It's so skinny," Aunt Beth murmurs.

"It really is kind of sad," Carrie murmurs.

"I think you picked the wrong sausage, Kee-Kee," Mom murmurs.

"This was the longest one I could find," Keanna explains.

"Maybe you could go shorter, but find more girth?" Gabby

murmurs, making me laugh. I can't argue, after experiencing the real thing. Thank God Chains is a big man, *everywhere*. I'm actually feeling pity for a damn sausage.

"What do you know about girth?" Aunt Beth asks Gabby. Gabby rolls her eyes, but she *doesn't* answer her mom.

"Dragon's cock makes that thing look like one of those BBQ wieners I fix in a crock pot."

"Mom!"

"I'm just saying, Kayden, that your dad is truly—"

"La La La La! I can't hear you!" I cry out so loud that I drown her out, praying I don't remember this conversation on my wedding night.

"Come on Kay-Kay, let's see if you can make Chains a happy man on your wedding night."

"He hasn't nutted in two weeks. All she has to do is sneeze to get the man off," Jazz mumbles, sounding bored, as she comes back into the room. I like Jazz, when you get her alone, she's kind of cool, but she really does try to be a bitch twenty-four-seven.

I take the poor, pencil thin kielbasa that's been stabbed by a fork. Poor thing. She should stab it a million times and put it out of its misery. I hold the fork up and sigh. It looks like I'm deep throating a needle thin kielbasa. I hold my head back and start lowering the sausage.

"We should have made them do the banana. I rocked the banana," Aunt Skye brags.

"Umm... you kept breaking it. I'm surprised poor Bull even lets you play," Mom laughs.

"He loves my mouth."

"Will you guys stop before I gag?" Jazz says and for once, I agree with her.

"What the fuck is going on here?" I hear Chains growl. I jerk my head up to look at him, and without thought, I bite the sausage off, leaving half of it on the fork, while trying to swallow the other half without choking to death.

"Mama, you touch that shit and you and me are going to have issues," Dad growls.

"Mi Cielo, what do you think you're doing?" Uncle Skull asks, his voice deceptively mild.

I ignore them all. I'm too busy chewing on a way too tough sausage, while staring into the eyes of my man. He's definitely pissed and I'm wondering just why that turns me on so much....

47

CHAINS

"Where are we going?" Kayden cries as I drag her through the strip joint.

"To the bathroom, where I can talk to you alone. Unless you want your parents to watch me spank your ass," I growl.

"I want to watch," someone yells out, but I don't look back to see who and I don't pay them a bit of attention.

"Will you slow down*!?!?*"

"No."

I finally spot the restrooms and make a beeline for it. I look at the men's room, but with my luck there will be men in there with all of their dicks out. With that thought in mind, I slap my hand against the door and push it open.

"Chains! You can't go in the Ladies Room!"

"Funny, I just did," I growl, finally letting go of her hand, but standing between her and the door. She's not getting away from me.

"Oh my God!" some woman almost screams, she grabs her friend and leans against the stall doors as if she's afraid I'm going to reach out and kill her. If her eyes get any bigger, I swear, they're going to burst out of the sockets.

"Rawr!" I snap like a lion.

Her and her daughter let out screams and run out the door.

"I can't believe you did that," Kayden says, looking at the door and back at me as if I've lost my mind—and maybe I have. "Are you insane?"

"If I am, it's because you've made me that way. What in the hell do you think you're doing at a damn strip club and just what were you deep throating when I came in?"

"I wasn't deep throating. The poor thing didn't even call for that, it kind of curled in my mouth. You know like you do when you're still asleep and not ready for playtime. Or you know, scared of my daddy."

"Kayden," I growl, my hand itching to spank her ass and show her just exactly what my dick can do to her.

"What? I'm just saying I thought I agreed to marry a man, but if you're so afraid of my daddy that little Chains can't come out and play...." She shrugs, not saying anything else and I narrow my gaze on her.

"You have about one-point-two-seconds to take that back and apologize before I show you exactly what happens when you piss off a man, Baby Girl."

"But are you a real man? I mean, I think you are, but it's been so long, I can't really remember."

"Kayden, I'm warning you."

"I'm going to go back out. The dancer Kee-Kee hired still owes me a lap dance."

"Baby Girl, if you try to take one step out of that door, I'll make you regret it."

"I doubt it. Daddy's outside and you wouldn't want to upset him," she says, sounding bored as hell.

"Try me."

"I believe I will," she says and then goes to walk around me.

"Don't test me, Kayden."

I let her get beside me, when she gets about two steps from the door, I grab her, pulling her roughly against me.

"And that, was the wrong decision, Baby Girl," I growl, my fingers thrusting painfully into her hair, as I pin her head back and force her to accept my kiss.

It's time Kayden finds out just what kind of man she belongs to.

48

CHAINS

I pull her against my body, her back to my front, my arm tight around her chest and my hand biting into her hip, not allowing her to move, even as she tries to get free.

I steer her toward the counter and line of sinks, the light bright and one of the mirrors reflecting her angry defiance.

"What do you think you're doing?" she growls, her eyes shooting fire.

"Teaching you a lesson, Kayden."

"A lesson? Who in the hell do you think you are Chains? This is not funny! Let me go. It's enough that you've probably given us seven years of bad luck!"

"What are you talking about?"

"Seven years of bad luck because you saw me before the wedding," she huffs.

"That's if you break a damn mirror, Kayden."

"Stick around. If you don't let me out of here, that's coming, Chains."

"The only thing coming in here is me inside of you and if you start being a little nicer, I'll let you come too."

"You're insane. We are not making love in a bathroom at a strip joint."

"You're right, we're not," I agree and watch her get this little wrinkle in her forehead.

"Then, what—"

"We're going to fuck, Baby Girl. I'm going to drill your sweet little pussy with my cock."

"I... uh... Chains, you can't do that here."

I tighten my hold on her hip, letting go of her hands at the same time, crowding her body with mine, making it still impossible for her to move. I lock my fingers into her hair, yanking hard enough to cause just a sliver of pain, and tilting her head back towards me.

"Put your hands on the counter, Kayden and bend over."

"No fucking way," she argues, but I can hear the breathlessness in her voice. I see the way her nipples pebble against the blue silk of her dress. My girl's not wearing a bra. She's going to get in trouble for that too.

I lean into her ear, nibbling on the shell, flicking my tongue inside it. I feel her body tremble against me and I don't even try to hide my smile. I look in the mirror, our gazes lock in the reflection and there's not a way in hell that she can disguise the fact that she's turned on right now.

It's radiating from her.

"Do it, Kayden. You don't have a choice. We both know you want my dick. That's what your little stunt tonight was about right? Pissing me off so I'd come down here and show you who you belong to?"

"I... Chains, we can't. I didn't mean for you to come here and..."

"Don't lie to me, Baby Girl," I warn her, letting go of her hair to let my hand trail down her back and over her luscious, thick ass. Jesus, she's got a fucking great ass.

"Okay. I did. I mean, not here. I thought if I pissed you off enough you'd be at my apartment waiting on me...but, we can't here, Chains. Anyone might come in. Jesus, my dad is outside somewhere."

"You can't play games with a man like me, Kayden. I'm not some lap dog that you teach to play fetch. I'm a man, Baby. Maybe you've forgotten that, but I'm going to take great pleasure in reminding you."

"Chains—"

"Now, put those pretty little hands on the counter and arch your ass out, Baby."

"I, Chains, let's think about this."

I scoot back and then slap her ass—not too hard, but hard enough she gets the message. I'm not sure how she will react to it, but she gasps and her body trembles. Her sweet little ass pushes against my hand.

Jesus, she just gets better and better...

"Now, Kayden."

She stares at our reflection. Her eyes are large in surprise, but smoky with desire, her breathing so ragged that I can hear it.

She slowly puts her hands on the counter, still watching me the entire time.

"Such a good little girl. Now tilt that pretty ass out against me, Kayden. Offer it to me."

"Oh God," she murmurs, licking her lips, as she does as I order.

"Not God, Baby. Just me. I own this pretty body now. I'm just going to have to remind you of that," I rumble against her skin, after I move her hair out of the way, kissing the back of her neck.

"Chains, let's go home. We can—"

"You aren't going to talk me out of this, Kayden. You wanted my dick and I'm going to give it to you—but I'm going to give it the way I want and *when* I want."

"But—"

I gather her dress up in my hand and pull it up over her ass.

She's wearing a damn thong and looking at the way her ass cheeks look separated by that thin line of fabric, it's a fucking wonder I don't come in my pants.

I let my finger move against the thin white line, then slip my finger under it and pull it tight knowing that puts pressure on her pussy. I can smell her desire. I know she wants this—wants me.

"Chains," she moans.

"I'm going to fuck you here, Kayden and you want me to, don't you?"

"What if someone comes in?" she whimpers. Her hips move as she tries to ride her damn panties. She's going to shatter for me and I'm going to enjoy every fucking minute of it.

I quickly undo my belt and the button and zipper on my jeans. I push them down on my hips, my hard cock falling out, the head already wet with my precum, the heated shaft, resting against her sweet ass.

"Then, they will know who you belong to, won't they, Kayden?"

"Chains," she whimpers as I slide my fingers back between her ass cheeks, and push against the small entrance there.

"You do belong to me, don't you, Baby Girl?"

"Yes," she says so softly that I can barely hear her, but there's a wealth of emotion in that admission.

"You're so wet, I could fuck your ass without doing much more than dragging it through your juices. You need my cock bad, don't you, Baby?" I ask her, as a drizzle of precum drips from the tip of my cock onto her ass. My balls tighten with the need to paint her sweet ass in my cum.

"I do, Chains. God, I do, but you have to hurry."

"What if I don't want to hurry, Kayden? What if I want to take my time and fuck you so slow that you'll think you are going to go insane before I finally let you come?"

"But, people... Chains, Jesus, stop toying with me."

"You still don't realize what I'm trying to teach you, Kayden," I tell her, my gaze watching as I let my fingers travel lower to her soaked little cunt.

"What..." she moans, her ass thrusting back toward me as the lips of her pussy quiver against my fingers.

"I own this pussy. I'm the only cock it's ever had. I'm the only man to tunnel inside your sweet little snatch and now you're shaped just for my cock."

I cup her pussy, her juices sliding down against the palm of my hand, her clit pulsating against my skin.

I gently squeeze her cunt with my grip, grinding her clit, as I rub my swollen cock against her ass cheek. It's torture, but so much fucking pleasure I groan.

"You're so full of yourself," she says, but she's whining the words out as she clenches her pussy tight, her body trembling underneath my hold.

"Soon you're going to be full of me and that's what you want, isn't it, Kayden."

"It's what you want, too," she says stubbornly.

I've already pushed her thong out of the way, and I decide to give her what we both want, mostly because I'm going to come if I don't. I take my cock in my hand and pump it once, letting more precum drizzle against her ass. Then, with one hand pressed on her back, and not a word spoken I make her open herself up for me. I line my cock up with her entrance.

"Hold on, Baby Girl. This is going to go hard and quick."

Then, I thrust inside of her, not stopping until my balls are pushing against her dripping wet cunt.

"Oh God, Baby. You feel so good," Kayden whimpers. "I've missed you so fucking much."

"I've missed you, too, Baby Girl," I growl. The pleasure is almost too much. I move out of her as slow as humanly possible, partly because I don't want to leave her body and partly because I love watching how her sweet honey clings to my shaft as I pull out.

Both hands grab her hips, harshly, holding her as I begin fucking her.

"This is going to be quick, Baby. Play with your clit if you need extra attention, I can't hold back," I order her, my voice sounding inhuman.

"I don't need anything except for you to stop talking and fuck me," she growls back.

I hold my body still, and just use my hold on her hips, using her body to fuck me, slamming her hard so her ass slaps against me and then, I pull her back until she's almost off my shaft—only to force her body to take all of me again.

Hard and quick, in and out, thrusting and pulling, slamming and receding, only to repeat.

Over and over, I fuck her, rational thought gone, just acting on instinct and pleasure. I can feel it starting, cum gathering, heated and so fucking full that it's almost as painful as it is pleasurable. I bite down on the inside of my jaw, using the pain to help me hold back until I can feel her begin to climax. Then, I let go, coming so hard in her that for a minute I'm afraid I might just pass out.

She cries out, coming so hard that her entire body quakes with it, vibrating against my body. I release jet after jet of cum, painting her insides so thick that it begins dripping out of her and against my shaft.

When I've emptied into her, I force myself to move. I'd rather stay inside of her for the rest of the night. That's not going to happen here, but I'm taking her to her place and fucking her again. She'll be lucky if she can walk down the aisle tomorrow. I'll carry her, though, if I need to. She's marrying me. There's no way that's not happening.

I lean over her placing a kiss on her neck, my gaze slowly raising to look into the mirror. I'm surprised to see her staring at me.

"I love you, Chains," she says, her voice soft, but full of emotion.

"I love you. No second thoughts, no teasing. You and I are forever, Kayden, nothing is changing that."

"I wasn't having second thoughts," she says, as I pull back, putting my somehow-still-semi-hard cock back in my pants. "I just wanted your cock," she says with a smile, pulling her dress down over her hips—just as the damn door opens.

"I can't believe you crashed a party. Jansen is going to kill me," a woman with long red hair says to an older woman as they walk inside.

"Oh, he will not. Besides, there are only two places open this late at night, honey. Strip bars, or a woman's legs. I'm hungry and I don't swing in one of those directions," the older woman says, and a startled laugh comes out of Kayden, even while she's doing her best to straighten her dress.

"I really should have gotten Petal to come back to Kentucky with me. I knew this was going to be a mistake," the redhead says.

"Oh my. Kentucky sure has some nice eye candy in their restrooms. Hello there, tall, dark and make my toes curl," the older woman says and Kayden does laugh then, curling into my body and her hand going down to zip up my pants.

Shit, I forgot about that.

"Oh God," the redhead says.

"Don't blame you for zipping that up, Darlin'. I would too if I was you. I haven't seen a specimen that fine since Chocolate Thunder."

"Uh...." Kayden says, and I figure she's like me, not sure what to say.

"I'm telling Jansen."

"Please do, it will make him take me aside and prove that he still has it," she says with a wink. "Are you giving private lap dances?" she asks me.

"Uh...." Shit, now I have no idea what to say.

"Only to me. I'm the bride to be they're having the party for and this is my fiancé, Chains."

"Chains? Damn that's a good name. The kind of name to make your female parts tingle."

"I'm sorry, she forgot her medication today," the redhead says, blushing.

"Oh please. You act like you're not the same woman who was banging my boy on the kitchen table at the farm last week," the old woman says.

"That's your fault. You and Jansen kept saying it was the best place to have sex."

"For us. You two sullied up our altar of thanks. Now we're going to have to find a new place to talk with the Lord."

"Whatever, Ida Sue. Maybe we should leave...," the redhead says, looking at me and Kayden.

"That's okay, we're about to go back out there," Kayden says, laughing.

"I'm afraid the sausage contest is over, I won. Some girl named Skye wasn't very happy about it. She was in the lead and kept muttering about how I ruined her chance at redemption. I think she might be a tick too tightly wound," the woman says and that's when I notice she's wearing a sash that says '*Deep Throat Queen.*'

"She'll get over it. It was... uh... nice meeting you," Kayden says, laughing and quickly leading me out of the bathroom.

"You too, and happy wedding!" she chimes as the door closes.

"There's some weird ass people here in Kentucky," I grumble.

"Do you think we can sneak out of here and go home, without anyone noticing?" Kayden asks, looking over at the party. They all seem to be laughing, but quite a few have left—most notably Dragon and Nicole. I can't help but be thankful for that.

"I don't give a damn if they notice or not. My cock is covered in your cum and I need more."

"Now, there's my man," Kayden purrs, as I lead her toward the door.

"Yeah, and you better never forget it," I tell her.

"I won't, besides you wouldn't ever let me."

For once, I can't argue at all with her. I'm in complete agreement. I'm never letting her forget that she belongs to me.

49

CHAINS

"You look good in a suit, Chains. Maybe you should give up the bike and be a banker," Dragon laughs.

I keep my eye looking at the doors to the Savage Clubhouse, looking for my woman to go through there and ignore my future father-in-law. I'm pretty positive that killing him would put a damper on Kayden saying I do and giving me a great wedding night.

"Nah, Dragon. I'm thinking he'd make a better insurance salesman," Gunner—who is *supposed* to be my best man—adds. I should have asked the Deep Throat Queen at the club last night instead. At *least* she seemed to like me.

"Fuck you both," I mutter. Which just makes them laugh.

"I better get. Time to go get *my* baby girl," Dragon says, slapping me on the back a little too hard. "Got to see if I can talk her out of this shit before it's too late," he adds with a wink.

God, he really is an asshole and he has no idea how much I'm worried that I am a mistake for Kayden. She deserves better and I don't feel anywhere close to what she deserves. Right now I'm feeling like a fucking duck out of water. It doesn't help that every motherfucker here is wearing jeans and their cut. I'm the only asshole in a suit. I wore it for Kayden though, because she's wearing her dream wedding dress. Her brothers told me that she always wanted a man that wasn't part of the club and kept going on about how her husband would wear a suit at their wedding instead of a cut. I won't ever be the kind of guy she dreamed of I guess, but I'm going to show her that I'll do my best to give her what she wants.

When the recorded music that comes over the outdoor speakers begins blasting, I feel my damn heart trip in my chest. First, her girl, Gabby comes out and Thomas meets her. She looks at him and seems surprised, but they walk up the aisle together, separating when they make it where I'm standing. Next, her mom is there wearing a light pink dress. Dom meets his mother and she takes his arm, kissing him on the cheek.

Dragon may be annoying as shit, and a thorn in my side, but I got to admit Nicole is gorgeous and probably too damn good for him. Then again, Kayden is too good for me too.

Her girl Keanna comes out next, and Dancer's boy, Hawk, walks her up the aisle.

"Get ready for my girl to rock your socks off," she says to me with a wink. I got to admit, I like that girl, even if she's crazy as hell.

That's when I see her.

Kayden.

Absolutely gorgeous in a long flowing white gown that curves against her body like a second skin. Her hair is piled up on her head with long curls hanging down on each side. There's no veil for my girl, instead a tiara and it's perfect, because she truly is a princess. I keep my eyes on her, she's smiling but as she goes to stand in front of me, I can see the tears. I know they're happy tears, but I don't want to see them on her face, just the same. I take the tip of my thumb and wipe away the couple of tears that have leaked out.

"No crying, Baby Girl."

"I love you, Chains."

"I love you," I whisper back.

"I'm starting to like you, Chains, but just so you know, if you hurt her even once, I'll kill you and do it with a smile."

"Daddy!"

"Understood," I tell him, and the strangest thing happens, because I do it smiling. I've never been surer of anything than I am of the fact that marrying Kayden is what I was meant to do in life. Me, a nomad, a man who has lived his life with no ties, drifting from town to town and loving that shit, was made for the sole purpose of marrying this woman, putting babies in her belly and making sure she spends her days laughing, smiling, and being happy. She's my reason, my purpose and I would gladly die to protect her and make sure she always has that.

Dragon kisses his daughter on the forehead.

"I love you, Princess. You're my heart and you always have been."

"I love you, too, Daddy."

"I'm always here for you, Kay-Kay. Even when you no longer need me. I will always have your six."

"I know, Daddy. You've always been there for me," Kayden says, crying again. She wraps her arms around him and he hugs her close and then fuck, if I don't see tears on his face as he holds his daughter close.

I've never been envious of a man in my life, but right now watching Dragon hold my woman and seeing the love between them, I am. I'd never tell the asshole, but I'm going to use him as a role model and one day, I'm going to hold my daughter in the exact same way and make sure she knows that I will always have her back. I will always be her safe place—just like I will always be Kayden's.

Dragon takes Kayden's hand and puts it over mine. The man looks me in the eye and I can see he's not one bit ashamed of the tears on his face. All I see from him right now is pride.

"I'm giving you my biggest treasure, son. Don't make me regret it," he adds.

My throat is tight as I nod my head, feeling so many different emotions that words are impossible. Then he walks away and I'm left holding Kayden's hand.

My lover, my best friend, my heart....

My destiny.

50

DOM

T*wo Weeks Later*

"GABBY, WE NEED TO..."

"Dom, don't... don't do this," Gabby whispers, her voice breaking.

Fuck.

I don't think I'll ever get used to how beautiful she is. Her almost porcelain white face, her golden blonde, wavy hair that falls around her face in a soft blanket. She's almost the spitting image of her mother, but even more beautiful. Then there are her eyes. She has those dark black eyes that have always called to me. Eyes that she says she got from her father, but I've never seen the likes of them before, anywhere. They seem to hold the secrets of the universe in them.

Shit.

There's never been another girl for me. I took one look at Gabby when I was a kid and that was it. I was gone for her.

Completely gone.

The problem is, so was my brother. I've spent my life looking out for Thomas. Hell, I still do—even though I don't have to. He's old enough and definitely tough enough to fight his own battles now. Still, this would hurt him and I can't do that... *Not even for Gabby.*

That doesn't mean this doesn't hurt like a motherfucker right now. I'd do anything to stop Gabby's tears. I'd lie, cheat, steal. Hell, I'd kill for this girl. I feel the same way about my brother, though and I can't hurt him. I just... *can't.*

I move my hand under her soft hair, curving it against her neck. I can feel her pulse pounding against my palm. I hate that she's upset. I hate those tears shining in her eyes even more.

"I have to, Babe. I don't have a choice."

"You do. We just tell Thomas that we truly love each other. He'll understand."

"He loves you, Gab. He will step aside, but if you don't think for one minute that it wouldn't gut him to see you with me every day, you're fooling yourself."

"Dom, you talk like he'll never find someone else to love."

"You're not that easy to replace, Babe."

"If I'm so special, why are you letting me go?" she says and more tears escape, sliding down her cheek.

I reach out to catch one of them, feeling as if my heart is breaking in two. This is not the way it was supposed to go. Thomas was supposed to move on once it was clear Gabby didn't have feelings for him. He was supposed to find someone he could love, someone that would make him forget Gab and then finally, her and I could come out with our relationship.

I've waited for that, for three years. Three years I've been sneaking and seeing Gabby any spare moment I got, biding my time until I could claim her as my own. I waited as patiently as I could, pushing girls—both good and bad—Thomas's way. Then everything changed two weeks ago.

Two weeks ago when Thomas walked into the garage at the clubhouse during Kayden's wedding reception and found Gabby and I making out. That's when everything became clear.

Crystal clear.

Thomas wasn't going to get over Gabby. He loves her, probably as much as I do. I can't claim Gabby like this. I can't rip my brother apart. I have to step away. I have to give her up.

"I have to look out for him, Gab."

"Bullshit."

"Gab—"

"Don't give me that, Dom. If you are breaking up with me, at least tell me the truth."

"I am, damn it."

"You're breaking up with me because you're constantly at the club now as a pledge. Hell, you live there. I'm not convenient anymore. You want your taste of club whores."

"It's not a damn fraternity, Gab. I'm not pledging. I'm working my ass off for the club as a prospect. I've got to prove myself to every fucking member of the crew. I'm not going to be handed the reins just because my old man is the President. They're working me ten times fucking harder, giving me every shit job there is, because *he is* my old man."

I'm so frustrated that she could even think this. I've tied myself into knots for years over her. If she thinks the club whores haven't already been throwing themselves at me, she's fooling herself. I haven't touched them, haven't touched anyone because Gabby is the only one I want.

"You can just—"

"And I don't want a fucking club whore. I've never wanted anyone but you. You know that shit. Don't you dare try and throw that shit in my face, Gabby."

"I'm just supposed to believe you? The great Dominic West doesn't lie, right?"

"Gabby—"

"What happened when you promised me that we'd face everything together, that it was you and me forever, Dom? Were you telling the truth then?"

"Damn it, Gabby."

"Just forget it," she says, the tears coming harder now. She pulls away from me and I let her go, my hand curling into a fist to prevent reaching out to grab her. "You just need to realize one thing, Dom."

"Gabby, baby..." I start and then just stop because I don't know what to say. I feel helpless.

Mostly because I am.

"You walk away from me now. If you insist on breaking up with me, when I walk out of those doors, you lose me."

"Gabby—"

"You're not just breaking up with me, Dom. You're giving me away to another man."

"Motherfucker, Gabby. I don't want you even talking to another man—"

"Then, stop me."

"Gabby..."

"Don't do this," she pleads.

"Damn it, Gabby. You have to understand," I growl.

"Don't do this, Dom!" she repeats. "Don't give me away! Don't break up with me."

"I don't have a choice, damn it. Don't you understand?"

"You have a choice, Dom. You're just making the wrong one," she whispers, backing away from me.

"Gabby, please, baby, try and understand."

"I love you Dom. I'm willing to tell my father, the one man in this world that I love as much as I love you, I'm willing to tell him to kiss my ass and that this is my life. I'm willing to do that *for you.*"

"It's not the same, Gabby."

"It's exactly the same. Tell your brother that this is our lives we're talking about and we love each other."

I want to... God, I do. She makes it sound so simple... but, I saw Thomas's face. I saw the pain. I heard him talking about her and I was there, after he found us together. I was there, trying to make him understand. I was there when for the first time in two years Thomas began stuttering with every breath.

I can't cause my brother that pain. I can't undo all of the hard work he's done. I can't hurt him like this... even if it means tearing myself apart.

"Gabby, I can't hurt him..."

"Yeah, I get it," she says, her voice so quiet I have to strain to hear it and the pain threaded into it is enough to bring me to my knees.

"Gabby."

"It's fine, Dom. You've made your choice. You can't hurt your brother," she says, using her fingers to wipe her tears away. It doesn't work, they're falling too fast, each one like a nail driving through my heart.

"Gabby, Baby..."

"You can't hurt your brother, you'd rather destroy me," she whispers and then, before I can stop her, she takes off running.

Running away from me...

And I let her go...

51

KAYDEN

"Promise me that we'll always be this happy," I murmur against Chains' chest.

We're lying in the bed in our private bungalow in Cabo. The breeze is blowing through the white gauzy curtains, the smell of salt air rolling in and you can hear the waves lapping lazily on the shore. If there is a heaven on Earth, then, this is definitely it. We've been here for two glorious weeks and tomorrow we head home. There's still so much up in the air about our lives there, but I'm not nervous about it. I know in my heart that everything will click into place. As long as Chains and I are together, that's all that matters.

"I can promise you that whatever happens, we'll always be together and I that I will always love you, Baby Girl," he says, his voice groggy with sleep and so sexy that my body instantly softens, wetness pooling between my thighs.

"I will always love you too," I whisper, squeezing him again and closing my eyes at the happiness that I feel rushing through me. I can hardly believe that this is my life now. That Chains is my husband. I always thought I wanted a man who was smooth and a business man, one who didn't understand the club life and wanted nothing to do with it.

I was obviously a fool.

"You better," he grumbles, kissing the top of my head.

"I don't want to go back to Kentucky."

"Well, as much as I'm dreading looking at your father again, we kind of need to. I need to get back and sort out my life. Plus, I want to take you and introduce you to my sisters. Let them see what a lucky son of a bitch I am."

"What if they don't like me?" I ask, genuinely worried.

"They will love you. Shit, Baby, have you ever seen one person that doesn't like you?"

"You'd be surprised," I laugh, rolling over on my back. "Can't we just find jobs here and live the rest of our lives as beach bums?"

"Well, that does sound good, but I think life's realties would intrude on us soon—not to mention your daddy if I don't get you back. Besides, I need to get my ass back to Kentucky and figure out what I'm doing."

"Are you going to regret giving up your old life, Chains? I know you said you were okay with it, but I can live anywhere with you, even traveling."

"That's not realistic, Kayden. You were made for a nice house, with kids playing in the front yard and a man who busts his ass to bring that to you."

"But this thing between us, heck us in general, Chains, it only works if we're both happy. It can't be all give and no take on your end, Sweetheart."

"Trust me, Baby Girl, I'm getting a lot. Just last night I got the best blow job a man could want. I bet you'd even give that sausage chick, that we met in the restroom, a run for her money."

I roll my eyes, but I do it laughing.

"Chains—"

He moves so that he's positioned over me, looking down at

me, his eyes so intense that there's no way to doubt the sincerity or the emotion in his next words.

"Kayden, I love you. I'd be happy anywhere as long as I knew you were. If you want to live on the back of my bike, traveling, we can do that. If you're happy, I'm happy. But, with you in my life, for the first time, I'm looking forward to putting down roots. I want us to have a family and one day I want to be the stupid motherfucker who makes sure my daughter gets a man she deserves and beat sense into him when he fucks up."

I laugh, I can't stop myself, as my fingers sift through the hair on his chest.

"Did you just call my dad stupid?" I giggle.

"You don't have to tell him that," he grouses.

"It will be our secret," I agree and I'm rewarded with his kiss. Once we break apart, I lightly rub his beard. "So, we're going to buy a house, are we?"

"Definitely. One big enough for all the babies I'm going to give you," Chains mumbles, moving down on the bed so he can kiss my stomach.

It feels so good that I move my hands up to his head, letting them play in his hair, my eyes closed and a smile on my face. He rests his head on my stomach and I can only think of one more thing that might make this moment perfect.

"That's probably a good decision, considering I'm late."

"Late?" he asks, his voice muffled because he's kissing my stomach. I look down at him, my beautiful, crazy, possessive man and not for the first time, think of how lucky and truly blessed I am to have found him.

"Late. I mean just by a week, but still, I'm always pretty regular and..."

"I don't understand, Kayden. What are you late for?"

"My period, Chains. I think I might be pregnant."

His body goes solid, his face showing shock and no other emotion at all. I almost get worried but then, a slow smile starts to form and his eyes deepen in color, to the point they almost glow as they sparkle down at me.

"You're pregnant?" he asks.

"I'm not sure, I mean, if I am, it'd be really early, but I'm late and I've never been late. I'm always regular like clockwork...."

"We're pregnant!" he shouts, kissing my belly again and making me laugh.

"Whoa, I told you I'm not sure yet, but yeah, there's a good chance I am."

"Chance hell, you're pregnant."

"Well, I guess I am then, if you say it's so, my husband."

"Damn straight," he mutters and then he starts kissing down my stomach and then lower, making me moan as his tongue licks against the lips of my pussy.

"What... are you doing?"

"I'm going to show my wife my appreciation for the two best wedding gifts she could have given me," he says.

"Two?" I ask, confused. I'm not truly paying attention, since his fingers are holding me open to him, and he just moved his tongue against my clit.

"First, she's giving me a baby...." He murmurs the words as he continues slowly teasing my clit, bringing my body awake with hunger and making me so wet that it'd be embarrassing if I didn't already know my husband was hard and wanting me just as much.

"And second?" I gasp feeling his fingers slip inside, my hips rocking gently, needing more.

"Second, I get to tell her dad that I knocked his baby girl up," he says and before I can laugh, or maybe even scold him, he quits torturing me and gets down to business with his fingers and that magic tongue he has. I forget about everything, other than one very important fact.

I'm a very lucky woman.

EPILOGUE

CHAINS

O*ne Year Later*

THE HOUSE IS quiet when I get home. That's not totally unusual, but lately Kayden has played soft instrumental music while she's working, because Little D likes it.

Detroit Weston Allen was born on a cold December morning and turned out to be the best Christmas present his mother or I could ever ask for. Every day with him is a new adventure and better than anything I ever knew existed. Kayden was worried I'd hate giving up life on the road, but I've never regretted it once. How could I? Not when I have her and Little D in my life.

I ended up joining the Savage Brothers. I didn't put it past Dragon—the asshole that he is—to take me in as a prospect, but he didn't. The fucker, actually had my cut and patch waiting on me when we got back from our honeymoon.

The bastard.

He gives me shit every so often, but I have to admit he's sharp as a damn tack and I really like him—when he's not irritating the crap out of me. I'm taking on more and more responsibility in the custom bike shop that we opened up. I enjoy it and working with bikes most days relaxes me. I do work for the club too, though Dragon doesn't ask a lot of me right now. We both agree that me being here for Kayden and Little D is more important. I imagine when he gets older that may change some, but I'll deal with it then.

I do like being a member of the club and if I'm honest, I like all of the guys. It's been a good fit.

But nothing is better than this.

I look at my gorgeous wife, lying on the bed, our son asleep on her chest and my heart swells with love and pride. I walk quietly into the room, taking our son in my arms. He doesn't make a sound, and I take him into his room, gently depositing him in his crib and switching on the monitor. I stare down at him, so full of pride that I could bust. He's everything good in this crazy fucking world and he and his mom are my reason for existing. I kiss him gently on the forehead, caressing his tiny fingers and watching as they curl around mine, even in his sleep. I don't know how long I stay like that, but eventually I make my way back to the bedroom, strip down and get in bed with my wife. It's too damn early and I'm too old for a nap, but I'd have to be stupid to pass the opportunity up. I lay down beside her, reaching at the foot of the bed and pulling up the folded blanket she keeps there.

We bought this house a couple of months after I joined the club. It's close enough to Dragon and Nicole's house that they are there if we need help with Little D, but far enough away that I get a break from my father-in-law too. Kayden has slowly made an empty house into a home. It's all one level with a big wrap around porch and it's huge—as in it has six bedrooms. I wanted one big enough so that all of our children had their own room. When I demanded six bedrooms with room to add on if needed, I thought Kayden was going to have me checked into the local psych center. It wasn't easily found, especially since I demanded all one level. I don't want my kids falling down the stairs, Kayden either. So when we found it, we paid way over what the asking price was, just so we didn't get overbid and lose out.

"I would yell at you for taking my snuggle buddy, but you make a pretty decent substitute," Kayden whispers softly.

"Glad you approve," I reply just as softly. Then, I set to work, pulling the dress off she's wearing.

"Chains, it's the middle of the day."

"And I want to nap with my woman and when we're in this bed together there's only one rule, remember?"

"Everybody must be naked," she mutters. "You really are crazy, you know that?"

"Crazy about you," I agree. "Now peel off those panties and hug up your man. Little D is sleeping now, but you know as well as I do, that might not last long."

She does as I ask, barely opening her eyes, and then snuggles against me. Her breathing evens out and I know she's already fallen back asleep. I tuck her in against me and just hold her, kissing the top of her head and thank the Man upstairs for the gifts that he's given me.

There was a time in my life, I had no direction and no plans. I saw a young girl that I shouldn't have even tried to touch and I immediately wanted her. When I found out she was the daughter to the most notorious MC President in this area, I knew touching her would only get me killed and drag her down into hell with me. It wasn't enough to make me stop—I had to have her. Now, here I am, after all this time, happy because I didn't take her down into hell at all. She grabbed my hand and my heart, taking me up—all the way to heaven.

And I'll never stop being grateful.

The End

* * *

Want to read more Jordan for Free? Turn the page!

JORDAN'S EARLY ACCESS

MAKE SURE YOU'RE IN THE KNOW!

Did you know there are three ways to see all things Jordan Marie, before anyone else?

First and foremost is my reading group. Member will see sneak peeks, early cover reveals, future plans and coming books from beloved series or brand new ones!

If you are on Facebook, it's easy and completely free!

Jordan's Facebook Group

*If you live in the U.S. you can **text JORDAN to 797979** and receive a text the day my newest book goes live or if I have a sale.*

(Standard Text Messaging Rates may apply)

And finally, you can subscribe to my newsletter!

Click to Subscribe

SOCIAL MEDIA LINKS

Keep up with Jordan and be the first to know about any new releases by following her on any of the links below.

Newsletter Subscription

Facebook Reading Group

Facebook Page

Twitter

Webpage

Bookbub

Instagram

Youtube

Text Alerts (US Subscribers Only—Standard Text Messaging Rates May Apply):

Text *JORDAN* to 797979 to be the first to know when Jordan has a sale or released a new book.

ALSO BY JORDAN MARIE

Savage Brothers MC—2nd Generation

Taking Her Down

Stone Lake Series

Letting You Go

When You Were Mine

Before We Fall

Savage Brothers MC—Tennessee Chapter

Devil

Diesel

Rory

Savage Brothers MC

Breaking Dragon

Saving Dancer

Loving Nicole

Claiming Crusher

Trusting Bull

Needing Carrie

Devil's Blaze MC

Captured—**CURRENTLY FREE**

Craved

Burned

Released

Shafted

Beast

Beauty

Filthy Florida Alphas

Unlawful Seizure

Unjustified Demands

Unwritten Rules

Unlikely Hero

Doing Bad Things

Going Down Hard—**CURRENTLY FREE**

In Too Deep

Taking it Slow

Lucas Brothers

The Perfect Stroke

Raging Heart On

Happy Trail

Cocked & Loaded

Knocking Boots

Made in the USA
Coppell, TX
10 January 2020

14341559R00138